4 DINOSAUR DETECTIVE

Out of Place

To Mr. Halloween—Happy Birthday. BBC

To Mary Jo, Murphy, and Seamus. DMD

4 DINOSAUR DETECTIVE
Out of Place

B. B. Calhoun

illustrated by Daniel Mark Duffy

Scientific
BOOKS FOR YOUNG READERS
American

W. H. FREEMAN AND COMPANY ◆ NEW YORK

Book design by Debora Smith

Scientific American Books for Young Readers is an imprint of
W. H. Freeman and Company, 41 Madison Avenue
New York, New York 10010

This book was reviewed for scientific accuracy by Don Lessem, founder of The Dinosaur Society.

Library of Congress Cataloging-in-Publication Data

Calhoun, B. B., 1961–

Out of Place/B. B. Calhoun [i.e. Christina Lowenstein].

—(Dinosaur detective ; #4)

Summary: When Fenton Rumplemayer's best friend, Max, comes to visit him in Wyoming, he doesn't seem interested in the puzzling dinosaur remains or the town Halloween party.

ISBN 0-7167-6543-8 (hard). —ISBN 0-7167-6551-9(pbk.)

[1. Dinosaurs—Fiction. 2. Paleontology—Fiction. 3. Friendship—fiction. 4.Halloween—Fiction. 5. Wyoming—Fiction. 6. Mystery and detective stories.] I. Title. II. Series: Calhoun, B.B. Dinosaur detective; #4.

PZ7.C127440u 1994

[Fic]—dc20

94-16079
CIP
AC

Printed in the United States of America.

10 9 8 7 6 5 4 3 2 1

1

Fenton Rumplemayer felt his right ankle twinge just a little as he climbed the last two steps of the staircase to the second-floor study. It was great to be out of his cast and off his crutches. Fenton had broken the ankle in a bicycle accident a while back, and for weeks there had been no running, no bike riding, and no playing fetch in the backyard with Owen, his dog. But worst of all for Fenton, there had been no visits to the dig site.

The dig site was on Sleeping Bear Mountain, a couple of miles from the house where Fenton and his father lived in Morgan, Wyoming. Mr. Rumplemayer, who was a paleontologist, had been sent out to Wyoming by the New York Museum of Natural History a few months earlier to head a team that was looking for dinosaur fossils. Fenton's mother was a paleontologist too, but she was spending a year traveling to dig sites in India.

Fenton loved digging for dinosaurs. In fact, he had already helped the Wyoming dig team with several important discoveries. And just as soon as his ankle felt strong enough for a bike ride, he'd be heading back out to Sleeping Bear again.

But right now it was eight o'clock, time for Fenton's weekly computer session with his friend Max Bellman back in New York. Saying good-bye to Max had been one of the tough things about leaving New York City. Even though Fenton had made two good friends in Morgan, Maggie Carr and Willy Whitefox, he still missed Max sometimes. The two boys had been best friends; they had been in the same class at school and had even lived in the same building. Now they kept in touch by computer modem; every Saturday night at eight o'clock they contacted each other to play Treasure Quest, the computer game that Max had designed.

Fenton looked at his watch: 8:02. He was two minutes late for Max. He hurried to the computer, turned it on, and activated the modem. One thing about Max—he was always on time, down to the minute.

Sure enough, when Fenton keyed in Max's number, Max was already waiting on his computer.

<HI FENTON. U R LATE, U NO>

came Max's greeting.

]HI MAX. YEAH, I NO. ONLY 2 MINUTES THO[

Fenton replied.

<THATS TRU. HOW R U?>

]OK. I GOT MY CAST OFF LAST WEEK. SOON I CAN GO
OUT 2 THE DIG SITE AGAIN[

<COOL>

]WHATS NEW IN NYC?[

**<NOT 2 MUCH. WE R GETTING READY FOR ENRICH-
MENT AT SCHOOL>**

]OH YEAH. ITS COMING UP SOON, RIGHT?[

Fenton had to admit, he kind of missed Enrichment Period. Every October the students at his old school, the Hibbs School in New York, had gotten a week off. They were supposed to use the time to do something different, to learn something new. Sometimes kids took special courses, or went on trips. Each student kept a journal based on something that he or she had experienced and shared it with the class when school started again.

]MY SCHOOL HERE DOESNT HAVE ENRICHMENT[

Fenton typed.

<Y NOT?>

]I DONT NO. SCHOOL HERE IS DIFFERENT. KIND OF
OLD-FASHIONED I GUESS. THEY DONT REALLY DO
ANYTHING LIKE THAT[

8

<WOW THAT STINKS>

]NOT REALLY. I MEAN ITS FUN IN OTHER WAYS. I CANT
EXPLAIN. WHAT R U DOING 4 ENRICHMENT THIS
YEAR?[

**<I CANT DECIDE. MAYBE GO 2 WORK WITH MY DAD
AGAIN>**

The year before, Fenton and Max had done their Enrichment Period at Max's father's computer software company. It
had been fun, spending the week with Max and his father and
learning about computers.

]IF I WERE STILL IN NY MAYBE WE COULD BOTH GO 2
WORK AT THE MUSEUM WITH MY PARENTS THIS YEAR
4 ENRICHMENT[

<2 BAD U R NOT HERE THO>

]YEAH. 2 BAD[

<WANT 2 PLAY TQ NOW?>

]OK[

Before long, the boys were involved in their game of Treasure Quest. Fenton didn't give Enrichment Period another
thought until it was time to sign off.

Then, suddenly, he got an idea.

]HEY MAX, MAYBE WE CAN STILL DO ENRICHMENT

TOGETHER AFTER ALL[

he typed.

<WHAT R U TALKING ABOUT, FENTON? U R NOT EVEN IN NY>

]EXACTLY[

<FENTON, U R NOT MAKING SENSE>

]MAYBE U CAN COME HERE 4 ENRICHMENT. U COULD COME 2 SCHOOL WITH ME + WE COULD GO OUT 2 THE DIG SITE WITH MY DAD + STUFF[

<COOL IDEA!>

]DO U THINK YOUR PARENTS WOULD LET U?[

<MAYBE. I COULD ASK>

]I BET IT WOULD BE OK WITH MY DAD. LETS BOTH ASK 2-NITE + SEE WHAT THEY SAY[

<OK. TALK 2 U LATER>

2

"Only two more days till Max gets here from New York," Fenton said happily as he, Maggie Carr, and Willy Whitefox pedaled their bicycles up Sleeping Bear Mountain Road, with Owen trotting close behind them.

It was the following Friday afternoon. The paleontologists had discovered a partially exposed dinosaur bone at the dig site, and Fenton, Maggie, and Willy were riding out to take a look at it.

"No kidding, Fen," said Maggie, pedaling alongside him. "You've only told us twenty-seven times since last weekend."

"Really," said Willy. "I can't wait to meet this guy."

"I've never seen you this excited about anything," said Maggie. "Except dinosaurs," she added. "Speaking of which, what about this new fossil your dad and the others found out at the dig site? Do they know what kind of dinosaur it's from?"

"Not yet," said Fenton. "They only discovered it yesterday afternoon, so there wasn't time to get it uncovered. They don't even know what part of the dinosaur's body it is."

"Wow," said Willy, "maybe there'll turn out to be a whole dinosaur buried there."

"I hope so," said Fenton, pedaling a little harder with anticipation.

"I guess it'll be cool for your friend Max to see it when he gets here," said Maggie.

"Yeah," said Fenton. "Max has never been to a dig site before. Too bad he can't bring his bike from New York. But I guess maybe my dad'll drive us out here."

"Or, if you want, maybe Max could borrow one of my family's bikes," said Willy.

"That would be great," said Fenton. "Thanks."

"You know, it's pretty amazing, if you think about it," said Willy, "that dinosaur bones can last all those millions of years."

"Well, it's the ground around them that preserves them," said Fenton. "If they were exposed for too long, they would just disintegrate."

"Kind of like mummies," said Maggie. "I'm reading this great book about ancient Egypt right now. It tells all about how they preserved the bodies of dead people and everything."

"I didn't know the sixth grade was doing Egypt," said Willy.

Willy was in the fifth grade at Morgan Elementary, a year behind Fenton and Maggie.

"We're not," said Maggie. "I'm just reading this book on my own."

Fenton wasn't surprised. Maggie was always reading. When he had first met her, he had been amazed by how much she knew about dinosaurs. It turned out that she had learned it all from books.

"Wow," said Willy, shaking his head. "I can't imagine reading *extra* like that." He grinned. "Unless it was a comic book, of course."

Fenton and Maggie laughed. Willy loved comic books. He had a huge collection of them that he kept in an old shack in the woods between his house and Fenton's.

A few minutes later they arrived at the dig site. They found Fenton's father and Charlie Smalls, another member of the dig team, studying a large rock that jutted out of the side of the mountain. Nearby sat one of the red tool kits where the paleontologists kept their digging equipment.

"Hi, Dad," said Fenton, climbing off his bike. "Hi, Charlie."

"Hello, son, Maggie, Willy," said Mr. Rumplemayer, looking up from his work. "Fenton, I hope you took it easy on the ride up here."

"Don't worry, Dad," said Fenton, reaching down to give Owen a quick scratch behind the ears. "My ankle's fine."

"All right," said his father. "I just don't want you to risk injuring it again."

"Hey, glad to see you back in action, Fenton," said Charlie. "You're just in time to get a look at this bone."

"Wow," said Fenton, walking over. "You mean you finished uncovering it?"

"Not quite," said Mr. Rumplemayer. "But we've got enough of it exposed now to identify it. It's a scapula."

13

"A scapula," said Maggie, "that's a shoulder bone, right?"

"That's right," said Charlie.

Fenton peered down at the long, narrow bone still partly embedded in the rock. It was about two feet long with one broad, flat end. He felt a shiver of excitement go through him. Chances were that this bone would lead them to others that were still in the rock. Dinosaur skeletons often lay buried for millions of years, until wind and rain finally wore away the dirt and rock that covered them. Sometimes only a small portion of a fossil became exposed, and sometimes it was more. Either way, an exposed piece of bone was an important clue to paleontologists trying to locate a dinosaur.

"What kind of dinosaur is it from?" asked Willy.

"We don't know yet," said Mr. Rumplemayer. "But I'd say it looks to be from some sort of biped."

Fenton nodded. He knew that the arm and shoulder bones of two-legged dinosaurs were usually slimmer and less sturdy than those of dinosaurs that walked on all four feet.

"We'll have to dig up a few more bones before we know what kind, though," said Charlie.

"Wow, cool," said Willy. "Do you really think there are more bones under there?"

"Let's hope so," said Charlie. "Meanwhile, we could use some help uncovering the rest of this one. What do you say, gang?"

"Sure thing," said Fenton happily. He headed over to the

tool kit, with Owen close behind him, and took out three small picks for digging.

"Hey, where's Professor Martin?" asked Maggie, looking around for the third member of the dig team.

"Oh, she's back at the trailer, analyzing some little mammal teeth we found near the bone," said Fenton's father.

"How come she's looking at those?" asked Willy.

"They provide a good clue to the age of the rocks, since we know a lot about how those teeth changed over time," said Charlie. "The sooner we know the age of the rock, the sooner we have an idea of the age of the dinosaur. And that can help us figure out what kind of dinosaur we have here."

"Let me just get a few measurements of this bone and the rock so I can start on a diagram," said Mr. Rumplemayer. "Then you kids can help Charlie uncover the rest of the scapula."

Fenton watched as his father measured the exposed area of bone, along with the surrounding rock, and wrote the figures down on a piece of paper. Fenton knew that paleontologists always made diagrams of the positions in which fossils were found. These diagrams could help them predict where more pieces of the animal might be buried.

Mr. Rumplemayer sat down a short distance from the rock and began to draw.

"Well, what do you say, gang?" said Charlie. "Ready to get to work?"

15

"Definitely," said Fenton, squatting down by the fossil with Maggie and Willy. It had only been a few weeks, but it seemed like a long time—way too long for Fenton—since he had done any dinosaur digging. It felt great to be back on Sleeping Bear Mountain with his father and the others.

Owen came over to his side, and Fenton felt the dog's warm breath in his ear.

"Okay, boy," he said. "You go lie down while we dig."

Owen trotted over to a bush and stretched out in its shade. Fenton had only had Owen for a few weeks now, and he was still amazed at how well the dog seemed to understand him. In fact, it had been Owen who ran for help the day Fenton broke his ankle.

Fenton, Maggie, Willy, and Charlie set to work chipping away the dirt and rock surrounding the scapula. Willy and Charlie dug at the broad end, the portion that formed the dinosaur's shoulder. Fenton and Maggie worked near the narrow end of the bone, the part that would have been attached to the animal's arm.

As always, Fenton was very eager to uncover the fossil, but he knew that working too fast could damage it. Digging up fossils was a long and painstaking process, and sometimes it was hard to be patient.

When Mr. Rumplemayer finished his diagram, he joined in the digging, and soon the scapula was almost completely exposed.

Then Professor Lily Martin arrived at the site. She was wearing her broad-brimmed straw hat, and she held an index card in one hand.

"Well hello, everyone," she said. "Fenton, it's nice to see you back up here on the mountain. How's your ankle feeling?"

"Hi, Professor Martin," said Fenton. "It's much better now, thanks."

"How's the analysis going?" asked Mr. Rumplemayer. "Do you have any information for us yet?"

"I certainly do," said Professor Martin with a smile.

"All right then, tell us," said Charlie, patting the scapula with his hand. "Just how old is this critter?"

Professor Martin looked down at her index card. "According to my analysis of the mammal teeth, the rock sample is approximately 115 to 120 million years old."

"Wow," said Willy. "That's old!"

"Well, I suppose that means we've got an Early Cretaceous dinosaur here," said Fenton's father.

"Cool," said Maggie. "I wonder which one it is."

Fenton thought about all the Early Cretaceous bipeds he knew of that had lived in western North America. There was the small, fierce predator deinonychus, whose name meant "terrible claw." And there was zephyrosaurus, the plant-eater from the hypsilophodontid family of dinosaurs. But both deinonychus and zephyrosaurus were too small to have had such a large shoulder bone. Maybe the scapula was from a tenontosaurus, a large, Early Cretaceous herbivore that could walk on either two feet or all fours. But he supposed there was really no way to tell for sure until they exposed more bones.

"Okay, come on," said Fenton, bending over the fossil again. "Let's get to work and see what else we can uncover."

"I'm afraid it'll have to wait for another day, son," said Mr. Rumplemayer. "It's getting rather late."

"Aw, Dad," sighed Fenton.

Charlie laughed. "If it were up to Fenton, he'd stay out here working all night."

Fenton laughed with the others, but he knew it was less of a joke than it seemed. He loved digging for dinosaurs. And if his father would let him, he probably *would* stay out there all night.

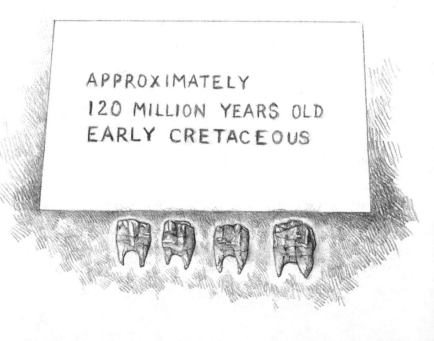

APPROXIMATELY
120 MILLION YEARS OLD
EARLY CRETACEOUS

3

"Wow, Fenton, this is so cool!" said Max, looking around Fenton's attic bedroom appreciatively. "It's got to be four times the size of your bedroom back in New York."

"Yeah, I know," said Fenton. "My favorite part is the windows. You can see in every direction around the house. It's almost like being in a lookout tower."

Max walked over to one of the tiny windows that were set into the attic's slanted ceiling and peered out.

"Sure is dark out there," he said.

"Yeah, I guess so," said Fenton. He had forgotten how bright it always was outside in New York. Between the lights from the buildings and the street lamps, the city was completely illuminated at night. Here in Morgan, most of the light came from the stars and the moon.

Max sat down on Fenton's bed, and Owen jumped up beside him and lay down.

"And you're so lucky you get to have a dog," said Max. "My mother won't even let me get a snake."

He reached out to stroke Owen's belly, and the dog rolled onto his back, putting his paws in the air.

"Yeah," said Fenton, "my parents always used to say no pets too. But now my dad likes Owen. And he says it's a lot easier to take care of a dog in the country. You know, since you don't have to walk him and stuff."

"Hey, yeah," said Max. "I never really thought of that. I guess he can just kind of walk himself, huh?"

"Sure," said Fenton. "Besides, Owen's outside a lot anyway. He pretty much goes with me everywhere. Except to school, of course."

"Oh, that reminds me," said Max. "On Friday, Mrs. Renner brought her pet ferret in. It was really cool. I got to hold it during Silent Reading Hour."

"Neat," said Fenton. Somehow he couldn't imagine Mrs. Rigby, his teacher at Morgan Elementary, ever bringing a pet with her to school. "We don't have Silent Reading Hour," he said.

"Really?" said Max, surprised.

"Yeah," said Fenton. "School here's kind of different from Hibbs. You'll see. I like it, though. Mrs. Rigby's really nice."

Mrs. Rigby was Fenton's favorite teacher. She taught sixth grade homeroom, as well as math and science. The sixth grade's first science project of the year, the Dinosaur Fair, had been one of the most fun assignments Fenton had ever had.

"What I really want to see is the dig site," said Max. "I'm

going to do my Enrichment Journal assignment on it. It sounds really cool."

"It is," agreed Fenton. "My father's team just discovered a new dinosaur there. They're not sure what kind it is yet, but they know it's from the Early Cretaceous."

"How can they tell that if they don't know what kind of dinosaur it is?" asked Max.

"Well, they dated some mammal teeth that were buried with it," Fenton explained. "And they turned out to be between 115 and 120 million years old."

"Wow," said Max. "This is going to be great for my project. I'm going to set the whole thing up on computer and write all about the dig site."

"Yeah, Sleeping Bear's really fun," said Fenton.

"Sleeping Bear?" Max repeated.

"The mountain," Fenton explained. "You know, where the dig site is. It's named after this rock near the top that looks like a bear. My friend Willy told me all about it. You'll meet him tomorrow, and Maggie, too."

"Willy's the one who played Treasure Quest with us, right?" said Max.

Fenton nodded. A couple of times Willy had been over when it was time to contact Max by modem, and Fenton had convinced Max to let him play too. "And Maggie was my partner for the Dinosaur Fair," he added.

"Oh, right," said Max. "You guys won, didn't you?"

"Actually, we came in second," said Fenton, thinking of the way he and Maggie had agreed to scrap their original idea and create a whole new project for the fair at the last minute. Changing their presentation like that had probably cost them first place, but it also helped them recover a missing bone from the dig site, so it was worth it.

"I wish Mrs. Renner would give prizes for the Enrichment Journals," said Max. "I bet I'd win one. I mean, I'm sure no one else is doing anything as exciting as visiting a real dinosaur dig site."

Fenton leaned back on his bed and sighed happily. This past week had felt like one of the longest of his life. It had seemed like Sunday would never arrive. But now Max was finally here. And Fenton would be able to show him the dig site and his school, and introduce him to Willy and Maggie. It was going to be great having Max in Morgan.

Max yawned.

"Wow," he said, looking down at his watch, "does your dad always let you stay up this late on school nights, Fenton?"

"What do you mean?" said Fenton. "It's not that late."

"Sure it is," said Max, showing Fenton his watch. "It's after midnight."

"It is?" Fenton glanced from Max's watch to the T-rex alarm clock on his night table. "No it isn't. It's only five after ten." Then he remembered something. "Your watch must still be on New York time, Max. You have to set it back two hours."

"Oh, right," said Max. He adjusted his watch. "There, five after ten." He yawned. "But how come I still feel like it's midnight?"

Fenton laughed. There was definitely something kind of strange about the two-hour time difference between New York and Wyoming. It was weird to think that just by hopping on a plane, Max had transplanted himself to a whole new time zone.

"Actually, I'm kind of bushed too," said Fenton. "Maybe we should go to bed."

"Sounds good to me," said Max, stifling another yawn.

Ten minutes later the boys were in their pajamas and ready for bed.

"You can have the bed if you want," said Fenton. "I'll sleep in the sleeping bag."

"Okay," said Max, climbing into Fenton's bed. "Maybe we can take turns. You can have the bed tomorrow night."

"All right," said Fenton. He crawled into the sleeping bag on the floor. "Here, Owen," he called, patting the space beside him. "Come on, boy, time for bed."

Owen made his way across the room, his nails clicking on the wood floor. To Fenton's surprise, he passed right by the sleeping bag and hopped up onto the bed.

"Hey, Owen," said Fenton, "I'm down here, boy."

"It's okay," said Max. He sat up and reached down to stroke

Owen's belly. The dog rolled onto his back. "He can stay here with me."

Fenton though a moment. It would be the first night that Owen hadn't slept with him. But he supposed Owen was more used to sleeping on the bed. Besides, maybe it would be nice for Max.

"Okay," he said.

Max reached out to turn off the light on the night table and lay down. "Night, Fenton," he said.

"Night, Max," said Fenton. "See you in the morning."

4

"Are you boys just about ready?" asked Fenton's father, finishing the rest of his coffee.

"Sure, Dad," said Fenton. He picked up his and Max's empty cereal bowls from the kitchen table, put them in the sink, and grabbed the two lunch bags on the counter. "Let me just go up to my room and get my backpack."

"Actually, I have to get something too," said Max, following Fenton out of the kitchen.

Upstairs, Fenton grabbed his stegosaurus backpack and slung it over his shoulder. He looked at Max, who was rummaging through his duffel bag on the floor.

"What are you looking for?" asked Fenton.

"A disk," said Max.

"A computer disk?" asked Fenton.

Max nodded. "I thought I should probably bring one with me to school. That way I can set up the format for my Enrichment Journal there and put it on disk so I can work on it here at your house too."

"Set it up at school?" Fenton repeated. "You mean on a computer?"

"Sure," said Max. "I'll just use one of the computers in your classroom."

"But there aren't any computers in our classroom," said Fenton.

"You're kidding, right?" said Max.

Fenton shook his head. "They're all in a special computer room. Our class goes there on Tuesdays and Thursdays."

Max looked amazed. Fenton knew what he must be thinking. At the Hibbs School, there had been computers in all the classrooms, and the students had been able to use them whenever they wanted. Sometimes Max had spent almost the entire day in front of a computer. Fenton knew Max probably wouldn't think too much of a school where he got to use one only twice a week.

But Morgan had other things that Hibbs didn't, Fenton reminded himself. Like a school yard where the students could eat lunch when the weather was nice. Eating outside was much more fun than eating in a cafeteria. And Morgan's gym was much bigger than Hibbs's. Max would see, when they got there.

"Well, I guess I'll just have to wait until tonight to set up my journal, then," said Max, zipping shut his duffel bag.

Fenton heard his father honk the horn out in the driveway.

"Come on," he said to Max. "We'd better get going."

They found Mr. Rumplemayer behind the wheel of the green pickup truck with the insignia of Wyoming State University on the door.

"I still can't believe this is your car," said Max, shaking his head.

"I know," said Fenton. "Isn't it neat? The museum gave it to my dad to use out here. Come on, let's ride in the back."

"What do you mean?" asked Max. "There's no backseat."

"No, back *here*," said Fenton, tossing his backpack into the bed of the pickup and hopping in after it. "Come on, Max. It's really fun."

"Well, okay," said Max. He pulled himself up over the rim of the truck. The engine started with a lurch, and Max grabbed on to the side as they pulled out of the driveway.

Fenton pointed to the mountains in the distance.

"That really tall mountain right there, the one closest to us, is Sleeping Bear, where the dig site is," he said.

"Oh," said Max. "Cool."

Fenton pointed to the roof of a yellow house that was visible above the trees. "And that's where Willy lives. Maggie's place is farther back up the road, toward the mountain. Her family owns a horse ranch."

Max looked around as the truck made its way into town. It had been dark when Fenton's father had driven them home from the airport the night before, so this was Max's first look at Morgan. Fenton watched as Max gazed silently at the tiny gas station, the barber shop, and the Morgan Market.

The truck turned a corner onto a side street, and Fenton pointed to a small red building.

"That place over there is really neat," he said. In front of the building was a weather-beaten, hand-painted sign that said WADSWORTH MUSEUM OF ROCKS & OTHER NATURAL CURIOS.

"That's a museum?" Max said incredulously. "It looks like somebody's house."

"Well, Mrs. Wadsworth does live there," said Fenton. "But it's a museum, too."

Fenton realized that Mrs. Wadsworth's museum might not look like much from the outside, but it was definitely fun inside. In fact, it was one of Fenton's favorite places in Morgan. The museum was tiny, but it was crammed full of interesting things that Mrs. Wadsworth had collected—teeth, bones, and skulls from animals, as well as feathers, birds' nests, and of course rocks. Fenton would definitely have to take Max to see it.

As they approached the school, Fenton heard his father toot the horn twice and saw Willy and Maggie on their bikes.

"Hi!" called Fenton, waving as the truck passed them.

Willy and Maggie waved back.

"That's them," Fenton said excitedly to Max. "That was Willy and Maggie." The truck lurched to a stop in front of the school yard. "Okay, this is it. We're here."

He grabbed his backpack and hopped out of the truck. Max climbed out carefully after him.

"Wow, Fenton," said Max, gazing at the red-brick building with its school yard filled with noisy kids. "So this is your school, huh?"

"Yeah," said Fenton.

For a moment he remembered how he had felt on his first day of school in Morgan. Everything had seemed so strange, so different from the way things had been at Hibbs. But now he felt completely at home at Morgan Elementary.

"Okay, boys," called Fenton's father through the window of the truck. "Have a good day."

As the truck drove off, Willy and Maggie rode up on their bikes.

"Hi, Fen," said Maggie, putting on her brakes. She climbed off her bike and turned to Max. "Hi, I'm Maggie Carr."

"Hi," he answered. "I'm Max. Max Bellman."

"And this is Willy," said Fenton.

"Hi," said Willy. "Actually, we sort of already met. Over the computer, that is."

"Oh yeah," said Max. "Right."

"That Treasure Quest sure is a cool game," said Willy. "Did you really make it up yourself?"

"Thanks," said Max. "Yeah, I designed it on my computer in New York."

"You know, there's a pretty cool game over in Fairpoint, at the mall," said Willy. "It's based on this comic book character called N-Force."

"N-Force is a video game," said Max.

"Oh, you know it," said Willy, grinning. "It's pretty good, huh?"

"Treasure Quest is a computer game," said Max. "There's a big difference."

"Oh, yeah," said Willy. "I guess so. But N-Force is a pretty cool character, either way."

"I'm not into comic books," said Max.

"Oh," said Willy, sounding a little disappointed.

"So, how do you like Morgan, Max?" asked Maggie, sliding her bike into the bike rack.

Max shrugged. "I haven't really seen it yet."

Maggie looked confused.

"Didn't you come down Main Street to get here?" she asked Fenton.

"Yeah," said Fenton. "Max, that was Morgan we just drove through."

"Really?" said Max, looking amazed. "There was hardly anything there."

"Well, it is kind of a small town, I guess," said Fenton.

Just then the bell rang.

"We'd better go line up," said Fenton.

"Yeah," said Willy. "We wouldn't want to be late. Max wouldn't want to get a demerit on his first day here."

"I'm sure no one would give Max a demerit anyway," said Maggie. "After all, he's just visiting."

"What's a demerit?" asked Max as they headed into the school yard.

"It's a bad mark against you," said Willy.

"Kind of like a strike in baseball," explained Fenton. "Except you get four of them instead of three."

"Four demerits and you have to stay after school for detention," said Maggie.

"You're kidding!" said Max. "What kind of school is this?"

"It's not like it sounds," said Fenton. "Hardly anyone ever gets detention."

"Besides," said Maggie, "you only have to worry about demerits if you do something wrong."

"Really, school's okay," said Fenton. "You'll see."

But Max didn't look convinced. And in a way, Fenton could understand. Morgan Elementary was definitely pretty different from Hibbs. At Hibbs, there hadn't been anything like demerits. In fact, there hadn't been very many rules at all.

"Come on," said Fenton. "We'd better go line up. See you at lunch, Willy."

"Okay, see you guys," Willy called, heading toward the fifth-grade line.

Fenton, Max, and Maggie joined the line of sixth graders and filed down the hall to their classroom, where Mrs. Rigby was standing behind her desk.

"Mrs. Rigby, this is my friend Max, who I told you about," said Fenton.

"Hello, Max," said the teacher. "Welcome to Morgan. I hope you enjoy your visit with us."

"Hi," said Max.

"Why don't you take a seat in the third row, next to Fenton," said Mrs. Rigby. "I've asked Ray to move over one desk to make room for you."

"Okay, thanks," said Max.

Fenton and Max made their way back to the third row, and Fenton took his usual spot next to Maggie. Max sat on his left, next to Ray Hitchins.

"Hi," said Ray, tilting back his cowboy hat and grinning.

"Hi," said Max quickly. He turned back to Fenton. "Do you always sit in exactly the same seats?"

"Sure," said Fenton. He thought of the way the kids at Hibbs were always scrambling for the best seats and trying to save the spots next to them for their friends. "Actually, I kind of like it this way."

Max shrugged.

"All right, everyone, time to settle down," said Mrs. Rigby. "Take your seats please."

"Where should we take them?" bellowed a voice from the back of the room.

Fenton didn't even have to turn around to know who it was. Buster Cregg was always making comments like that. And now, as usual, his friends Matt Lewis, Jen Wilcox, and Jason Nichols were laughing hysterically at his joke.

Maggie looked at Fenton and rolled her eyes. Fenton nodded back at her. Maggie and Fenton both thought that Buster was the most obnoxious kid in school. And he wasn't too fond of them, either, especially since they had exposed him as a cheat and a thief back at the beginning of the year.

"Who is that guy?" said Max under his breath.

"That's Buster," Fenton whispered. "The biggest jerk in school."

"All right, Buster, that's enough," said Mrs. Rigby sternly. "Now, class, I'd like you to all settle down so I can take the roll."

"Where are you going to take it?" cracked Buster.

Again, Matt, Jen, and Jason started laughing.

"Buster, I'm warning you," said Mrs. Rigby, angry now. "Another word out of you and you're getting a demerit."

Buster was silent.

Max looked at Fenton and raised his eyebrows.

"I thought you said no one ever gets demerits," he said.

"I said hardly anyone ever gets detention," Fenton whispered. "But I should have said except Buster. He's always in trouble."

After Mrs. Rigby finished the roll, she said she had an announcement to make.

"As you all know, Halloween is coming up," she began.

Fenton leaned toward Max.

"When's Halloween?" he whispered.

"October thirty-first," said Max.

"I know," said Fenton, "but when is that?"

Max shrugged. "Sometime next week, I think."

"As usual," Mrs. Rigby went on, "there will be a big Halloween party over at the Morgan firehouse."

There were several murmurs of excitement. Fenton turned to Maggie.

"When's Halloween this year?" he asked.

"A week from tomorrow," she answered. "Tuesday. But they always have the party on the weekend. It's really fun."

"All right, everyone, quiet down, please," said Mrs. Rigby.

Fenton glanced at Max. Max was due to leave on Sunday, two days before Halloween. But if what Maggie was saying was true, maybe he'd still be here for the party.

"Now," said Mrs. Rigby, "as some of you may already know, the town of Morgan is also celebrating its one hundred and twenty-fifth anniversary this November. So, in honor of the occasion, Fire Chief Gonzalez has asked me to tell you that this year's party is going to be bigger and better than ever. This year there's going to be live music, and in addition to the regular games, there will be a costume contest."

The murmurs grew louder as students began to whisper excitedly.

"Is there a prize?" asked Franklin Lee.

"Yes, there is," said Mrs. Rigby. She picked up a stack of papers from her desk. "Now, all the information is right here on these flyers I'm going to pass out." She handed the papers to Lisa Levine in the first row.

As the stack of flyers made its way back to his row, Fenton turned to Max.

"Maggie says they always have the party on the weekend," he said. "So maybe you'll still be here."

"Did Mrs. Rigby say the party was in a firehouse?" said Max, screwing up his face a little.

"Uh, yeah, I think so," said Fenton.

"Isn't that kind of weird?" asked Max.

"I don't know," said Fenton. "I mean, I guess there aren't too many other places in Morgan big enough for a party like that."

Maggie tapped Fenton on the shoulder and passed him the flyers. Fenton took one and began to read.

Calling All Ghouls, Goblins, & Ghosts

**The Annual Morgan Firehouse Halloween Party
Saturday, October 28**

* * *

Come celebrate Morgan's 125th Anniversary
with live music, potluck refreshments,
candy, games, & a costume contest.

Prize for the most original & convincing costume:
regulation-sized Ping-Pong table
(donated by Harrison's Hardware & Sporting Goods).

Fenton turned to Max.

"Hey, the party's this Saturday," he said, "the night before you leave, Max. That means we can go together."

"Yeah, I guess," said Max, looking down at his flyer.

"Wow, this is great," said Maggie, reading her own flyer. "A Ping-Pong table."

"Yeah, I know," said Fenton. "Wouldn't that be cool?"

"Definitely," agreed Maggie. "We should all try to come up with some really good costumes."

"That's for sure," said Fenton.

He looked down at the flyer and thought back to all the Halloweens he and Max had spent together in New York, trick-or-treating in their building. Their first year, when they were only six, they had gone as robots. Max's mother had helped them make the costumes out of cardboard boxes, and they had practiced saying "Trick or treat" in mechanical voices for a week beforehand. And then there had been the year they had both been vampires, with big fangs and long black capes. This year would have been the first Halloween he and Max had spent apart. But now it didn't have to be. Now they could plan their costumes together again as always, and on top of it all, they even had a chance to win a Ping-Pong table!

5

When the sixth grade got out to the school yard for lunch later that day, Fenton, Max, and Maggie found Willy sitting in his usual spot on a patch of grass, reading a comic book.

"Wow," said Max they sat down on the grass next to Willy. "This is great. Do you guys always get to eat outside?"

"As long as it stays warm," said Maggie, pulling her sandwich out of her paper bag. "Why, you guys never ate outside in New York?"

Fenton shook his head.

"There was nowhere outside to eat," he explained.

"Gee, I can't imagine that," said Maggie. "I hate it when it gets cold and we have to eat in the cafeteria."

"Our school in New York has other really great stuff, though," said Max.

"You mean *your* school in New York," Maggie corrected. "This is Fenton's school now."

Max shrugged. "I guess."

Fenton decided to change the subject.

"Hey, Willy," he said, "did you hear about the Halloween party?"

"Sure," said Willy, taking a bite of his peanut butter and jelly sandwich. "My dad's one of the people in charge of it."

"Really?" said Fenton, surprised.

"Willy's father's a firefighter," said Maggie, biting into her chicken salad sandwich.

"I thought your father was an electrician," said Fenton.

"He is," said Willy. "But he's also a member of the volunteer fire department."

"What's a volunteer fire department?" asked Max.

"Morgan's too small to have full-time firefighters. So lots of grownups in town volunteer. They learn what to do, and then when there's a fire, they all work together to put it out," explained Maggie.

"Right," said Willy. "Like my dad's on call on Mondays, Tuesdays, and Thursdays. That means if there's a fire then, he helps put it out. He has this really cool flashing light to put on his car, but he's only allowed to use it if there's a fire."

"Oh," said Fenton. "We didn't have that in New York. At least, I don't think so."

"We don't need that in New York," said Max. "We already have a huge professional fire department."

"Oh yeah," said Fenton. "I guess you're right."

"Anyway, my dad always helps out with the Halloween party," said Willy. "He rigs up the lights in the stalls for the games—you know, like the bean-bag toss and bobbing for apples and stuff."

"Bean-bag toss?" repeated Max. "Bobbing for apples? Isn't that for little kids?"

"Well, the really fun part this year's going to be the costume contest," said Maggie. "Imagine winning a Ping-Pong table!"

"What are you going to be, Maggie?" asked Willy.

"I don't know yet," she answered. "I want to think of something really good. How about you?"

"Maybe I'll go as someone from a comic book," said Willy. "Like Lazer—he's half man and half rocket. Or Dr. Smoke—he can turn himself into a vapor."

"A costume to make you turn into a vapor could be kind of hard to do," said Maggie, laughing. She turned to Fenton and Max. "What about you guys?"

"I don't know," said Fenton. He turned to Max. "What do you think we should be?"

Max shrugged. "I don't know. Are you positive you really want to go to this party?"

"Sure," said Fenton. "It sounds fun."

"Yeah, this year it's supposed to be really good," said Willy. "My dad said they're doing a lot of extra stuff for it, since it's also Morgan's hundred and twenty-fifth birthday."

"That's right," said Maggie. "This November it'll be exactly one hundred twenty-five years since Morgan was founded."

"Thanks to Mighty Morgan," said Willy.

"Mighty Morgan?" said Fenton. "Who's that?"

"He's the guy they say saved the lives of the settlers who ended up founding the town of Morgan," said Maggie.

"Right," said Willy. "Mighty Morgan was seven feet tall, and he had a beard that was two feet long. He was a trapper who lived in the mountains around here, and they say he once killed a bear with his bare hands."

"Come on," said Max. "You're kidding, right?"

"No," said Willy. "It's all true. He was half Arapaho, you know."

"What's that?" asked Max.

"Arapaho Indian," explained Fenton. "Native American. Willy's family is Arapaho. So go on, tell us the story."

"Well," said Maggie, "supposedly, a hundred and twenty-five years ago this group of settlers was headed west to California when there was a huge blizzard, and they were stranded at the foot of Sleeping Bear Mountain. According to the legend, Mighty Morgan is the guy who saved them."

"It wasn't just a blizzard," Willy corrected. "There was an avalanche, too. You see, everyone was huddled together in one wagon to stay warm, and they were trapped in there by the avalanche. When Mighty Morgan saw the other wagons outside and the huge pile of snow, he realized what had happened. He tunneled through fifty feet of snow single-handedly and saved the settlers' lives."

"No way," said Max. "That's impossible."

Willy nodded. "It's all true. And after he saved their lives, they decided to settle right here, and they named the town of Morgan after him."

"Supposedly they even offered to make Mighty Morgan their first mayor," said Maggie. "But he said no, he'd rather just return to the mountains."

"Wow, that's some story," said Fenton.

"It sure is," said Max. "A made-up story, I'd say."

"I'm telling you, it really happened," Willy insisted.

"Oh, come on," said Max. "Killing a bear with his bare hands? Tunneling through fifty feet of snow? You don't expect me to believe that, do you?"

Suddenly Fenton felt uncomfortable. It almost seemed like an argument was about to break out. To his relief, Maggie changed the subject.

"Hey, maybe while Max is here you guys should all come out to the ranch," she said. "We could go riding."

"Riding?" Max repeated.

"Sure," said Maggie. "Horseback riding."

"Cool," said Fenton, excited. He had never been horseback riding before, and he knew Max hadn't either.

"Thanks anyway," said Max, "but I'm not really into horses."

Fenton looked at Max. What was wrong with him? He was acting like a real stick-in-the-mud. First about the party, and now this. How could he possibly know that he wasn't going to

42

like something if he wasn't even willing to give it a try?

Maggie sighed a little.

"So then, what *do* you like to do, Max?" she asked. "What do you do for fun in New York?"

"New York's the greatest," said Max. "We've got everything there. In fact, there's this great new movie theater that just opened three blocks from Fenton's and my—I mean, my—building."

"Oh yeah?" said Fenton. It was kind of weird to think of something new opening in his old neighborhood.

"Yeah, you don't know what you're missing," said Max. "It's got eight screens, and this special sound system called 'Realoud' that makes it sound like you're right there *in* the action."

"Cool," said Willy appreciatively.

"You know that new racing movie, *Wild Wheels?*" said Max. "I just went to see it there, and it was practically like being in a race car."

"Sounds fun," said Fenton.

"It's a great movie," said Max. "Have you seen it?"

"Not yet," said Fenton.

"It hasn't come to Morgan," explained Willy.

"Not to *any* of the theaters?" asked Max incredulously.

"There's only one theater in town, the Morgan Cinema," said Maggie.

"You're kidding!" said Max. "Wow, that stinks."

"It's not so bad," said Fenton. "I mean, it's a fun theater. They show cartoons before the movie, and they have really good popcorn."

Max looked unconvinced. Cartoons and popcorn probably didn't sound so great compared to eight screens and "Realoud" sound, Fenton realized.

"Anyway," said Fenton, "there's other stuff to do in Morgan besides go to the movies."

"Like what kind of stuff?" asked Max.

"Outdoors stuff," said Fenton.

"Like riding bikes and playing Frisbee," said Willy.

"And going to the dig site," Maggie added.

"I'm definitely into going to the dig site," said Max.

"Yeah," said Fenton, relieved that they were finally talking about something Max seemed interested in. "It's probably the most exciting time to go there, too. You know, with the new find and everything. Maybe they'll even be able to identify the dinosaur while you're here, Max."

"I sure hope so," said Max. "It would definitely be good for my project."

"Max is doing a project on the dig site for school," Fenton explained to the others.

"Really?" said Maggie.

"That's right," said Max. "For Enrichment."

"Oh yeah," said Willy. "Fenton told us about that. I can't believe you really get a whole week off from school."

"I know," said Max, beaming. "Hibbs is the greatest."

"Oh, by the way, Fenton," said Willy, "I asked my mom, and she said it would be fine for Max to borrow a bike."

"Great," said Fenton. "Thanks a lot."

Just then the bell rang.

"Why don't you all come over after school," suggested Willy, standing up. "We can all plan our costumes together and Max can get the bike."

"Okay," said Maggie.

"Sounds good to me," said Fenton. "Okay with you, Max?"

"Sure," said Max, shrugging. "I guess so."

But Fenton couldn't help noticing that Max didn't look very enthusiastic at all.

6

"Let's stop home and get Owen first," said Fenton as he and Max made their way up the road after school that day.

"Okay," said Max, panting a little. "Gee, it's too bad your father couldn't pick us up in the truck."

"Yeah, well, he's out at the dig site," said Fenton. "But now that Willy's lending you a bike, we can ride to school and back every day."

"Yeah, I guess," said Max.

"And this way we can go out to the dig site any time we want," said Fenton.

Max looked up at the mountain. "Isn't it kind of far to ride a bike?"

"Nah," said Fenton, turning up his driveway. "I mean, sure, it's tougher going up the mountain than it is coming back down, but it's a fun ride. You'll see."

"I guess," Max said again.

Fenton opened the door to the house, and Owen came bounding out to greet them. After jumping up and putting his paws on Fenton's chest, tail wagging, the dog hurried over to Max and rolled over on his back.

"Boy, he sure seems to like that," Fenton commented, watching as Max rubbed Owen's belly. "Okay, come on, boy, we're going to Willy's."

Owen jumped up, wagging his tail, and headed off in the direction of the woods behind the house.

"See how he understands everything I say?" said Fenton proudly.

"Yeah, Owen's a great dog," agreed Max.

They made their way through the woods toward Willy's backyard, where they found Willy and Maggie tossing a Frisbee.

"I got it! I got it! I got it!" Maggie yelled. She ran backward, her arm extended toward the Frisbee flying through the air, and smashed right into Fenton and Max.

"Oops," she said, stumbling. "Sorry about that."

"That's okay," said Max, regaining his balance.

"Come on," yelled Willy from the other end of the yard. He pointed to the Frisbee at Max's feet. "Throw it back this way."

Max bent down, picked up the Frisbee, and tossed it toward Willy, with Owen chasing after it. It was a couple of feet short, but Willy ran for it and made a diving catch.

"Nice one, Willy," said Maggie as Willy trotted toward them, the Frisbee in his hand and Owen following along behind him.

"Thanks," he said, flipping it to her. "Hi, you guys. Here's the bike." He gestured to a large black three-speed bike with a basket on the handlebars that was leaning against the side of the house.

"*That?*" said Max.

"It's all we have," said Willy. "It's my mom's. My dad's bike has a flat."

"Hey," said Fenton, "it's a bike. That's what matters, right?"

Max didn't say anything.

"Thanks, Willy," said Fenton.

"No problem," said Willy. "Hey, guess what? I decided what I'm going to be for Halloween."

"Let me guess," muttered Max. "A comic-book character."

"Right," said Willy, grinning. "His name's Eon, and he's a time traveler. He can fly into the future and the past."

"Sounds neat," said Maggie.

Just then the back door to Willy's house opened, and his little sister, Jane, came out, a wooden recorder in her hand.

"Hi, Fenkon," she said. "Do you like my new recorder?"

"Yeah, Jane, it's great," said Fenton, wondering if Jane would *ever* get his name right. "Can you play it?"

"Oh, no," moaned Willy. "I wish you hadn't said that."

"I'm trying to learn," said Jane, sitting down on the back step and taking the recorder in both hands.

"And the rest of us are trying not to listen," said Willy.

Jane scowled. "I can play okay. Sort of." She raised the instrument to her mouth and began to blow, moving her fingers over the holes. A few squeaky notes came out.

"Hey, can I see it?" asked Max, putting out his hand.

"Jane, this is my friend Max from New York," Fenton explained.

"Well, okay, if you're Fenkon's friend," said Jane, handing over the recorder.

Max brought the recorder to his lips and played a quick tune.

"Hey, that sounded pretty good," said Maggie.

Fenton wasn't surprised. Max had been playing the clarinet since he was six years old. He could play the saxaphone and even the trombone a little, too. The recorder must be pretty similar in some ways.

"Yeah," said Willy. "A lot better than you, Jane."

Jane pouted. "How come it doesn't sound like that when I play it?"

"Well, here," said Max, holding out the recorder. "First of all, you're not covering the holes. See how I do it? You have to use the fleshy part of your fingers and press pretty hard."

Jane took the recorder.

"Like this?" she said, placing her fingers on the holes.

"That's right," said Max. "Now take a deep breath, all the way into your belly, and kind of let it out easy."

Jane blew two long, steady notes, pulled the recorder away from her mouth, and smiled.

"There," said Max. "That sounds better already."

Jane put the recorder back to her lips and played the notes again.

"Hey," said Maggie, tossing the Frisbee in the air. "Are we going to play, or what?"

"I've got a better idea," said Willy. "Let's all go to the shack."

"What's the shack?" asked Max.

"It's kind of like my clubhouse," said Willy.

Jane put the recorder down.

"That's no fair," she whined. "You can't leave now; Max is teaching me."

Max leaned toward her. "Hey, you practice that stuff for a little while, and later on I'll show you how to play a real song, okay?"

"Well, all right," she answered.

Maggie tossed the Frisbee onto the grass, and the four of them set off through the woods behind Willy's house, with Owen following close behind them.

"Hey, now I can show you guys Eon, the guy I'm going to be for Halloween," said Willy as they approached the clearing where the shack stood.

"Oh, yeah," said Fenton. "We still have to figure out our costumes for the Halloween party, Max."

"I don't know about this party, Fenton," said Max, looking doubtful. "Wouldn't you rather just go trick-or-treating?"

"There isn't really any trick-or-treating in Morgan," said Maggie as they stepped into the shack.

Fenton looked at her in surprise. That seemed a little odd. "There isn't?"

She shook her head. "That's one of the reasons the firehouse gives the party every year, so kids will have something to do."

"That's right," said Willy, sitting down on one of the empty crates that were littered around the shack. "You see, a few years ago on Halloween a bunch of kids were pulling a prank and they ended up setting fire to someone's garage. That's how Fire Chief Gonzalez got this idea for the Halloween party."

"Oh," said Fenton. "I guess that makes sense."

"Not to me," said Max, taking a seat. "No trick-or-treating. What a raw deal."

"Not really," said Maggie. "I mean, my older sister, Lila, used to go trick-or-treating in town before all this happened, and she says the firehouse parties are definitely better; they have bowls of candy out all over the place, so you actually end up getting more candy this way."

"Hey, Fenton," said Max, reaching down to rub Owen's belly. "Remember how much candy we always get back in New York? How we have to stop home and dump out our bags a bunch of times?"

Fenton nodded. The apartment building he had lived in had been twenty stories tall, and there had been lots of doorbells to ring on each floor.

"So, Willy," he said. "I thought you were going to show us what this Eon guy looks like."

"Oh, yeah," said Willy. He rifled through a stack of comic books on the floor. "Here, this is him."

The cover of the comic book showed a figure in a bright orange suit and mask with silver wings on the backs of his feet. He had one arm extended, the hand curled into a fist, and he was bursting through the face of a giant clock. Stacked around the edges of the clock were bars of gold, and written across the top of the page in bright gold letters was the title: "Eon & the Mines of King Tut."

"Hey, let me see that!" said Maggie, reaching for the comic book. "Wow, I was just reading about Tutankhamen."

"Oh, boy," said Willy. "Here we go with the Egypt stuff again."

"Hey," said Maggie, looking through the comic book. "This isn't right. They're showing Tutankhamen as an old man here, but he actually died when he was still young." She put down the comic book. "Did you guys know that the ancient Egyptians believed that their rulers, the pharaohs, were gods?"

"Sure," said Max. "They called them 'living gods.'"

Maggie looked at him, surprised.

"Yeah," she said. "That's right."

"And some of them became rulers when they were just little boys," said Max.

54

"Actually, there was one woman pharaoh, you know," said Maggie.

"Oh, you mean Cleopatra?" said Max.

"No," said Maggie. "Cleopatra wasn't a pharaoh. I'm talking about Hatshepsut."

"*Who?*" asked Willy.

"Hatshepsut," said Maggie again. "She was the stepmother of Thutmose III, but he was too young to rule, so she took over. She built Egypt's tallest obelisks."

"What's an obelisk?" asked Willy.

"The Egyptians built them as religious symbols," said Maggie. "They were these tall, thin, stone things with a point at the top. You know, like the Washington Monument."

"Or Cleopatra's Needle," said Max.

"That's an obelisk in Central Park in New York," Fenton explained.

"Well, Hatshepsut's obelisks were 97 feet tall," said Maggie. "And they weighed 320 tons each."

"Wow," said Fenton. "This Hatshepsut sounds like she was pretty cool."

"Yeah," said Maggie. "Hey, I know—maybe I'll be Hatshepsut for Halloween."

"But who's even heard of her? No one will even know who you're supposed to be," said Max.

"So?" said Maggie, shrugging. "I will."

"Hey, Maggie," said Willy, grinning. "If you're Hat-, Hat-,

whatever her name is, and I'm Eon, I can fly back in time and visit you."

"Yeah," said Fenton, "and while you're at it, Eon, maybe you could fly back to the Early Cretaceous and find out what kind of dinosaur my father and the others are working on out at the dig site."

"When do you think they will figure out what kind it is?" said Max.

Fenton shook his head. "I don't know. Sometimes it takes quite a while to get enough bones uncovered to figure that stuff out, Max."

"Well, I hope it doesn't take *too* long," said Max. "For the sake of my Enrichment Journal project."

"What exactly are you doing for your project?" asked Maggie.

"Well," said Max, looking excited, "I'm going to set the whole thing up on the computer. I thought I'd create a format that looked just like a loose-leaf notebook on the screen, with a cover, and pages you can turn by using the mouse."

"I don't get it," said Willy. "Why don't you just use a real notebook?"

Max stared at him. "Why would I want to do that when I can use a computer? Besides, you can do so much more with a computer. Like program it to turn to any page instantly. Or automatically enter the date for you. Or use sound. Hey, maybe I'll set it up so it plays a little tune every time you turn a page."

"Oh," said Willy.

"Sounds interesting," said Maggie. "There's just one thing I don't understand."

"Sure," said Max. "What is it?"

"What exactly does all that have to do with the dig site?" she asked.

Fenton couldn't help smiling a little. He had just been wondering the same thing.

7

"So, how far away is this dig site?" asked Max as he and Fenton pedaled up Sleeping Bear Mountain Road the following afternoon after school.

"Oh, just a couple of miles," said Fenton, turning his head to check on Owen, who was trotting behind him.

"A couple of miles?" said Max.

"Yeah," said Fenton. "Don't worry; it's not really as far as it sounds, Max. You'll see."

But Fenton was beginning to have his doubts. Taking the bikes and heading out to the dig site after school had seemed like a good idea at first. But the road had barely begun to climb uphill, and Max was already breathing pretty heavily. Plus, he was wearing his loafers, the only shoes he had brought with him from New York, and his feet kept slipping off the pedals. Fenton realized that he probably should have lent Max a pair of his sneakers, but it was too late now.

"Okay, now we go this way," said Fenton, turning off the

paved road and onto the dirt one.

Max skidded a little as he made the turn.

"Is this a real road?" he asked, gripping his handlebars as the bike bounced over the dirt and rocks.

"Sure," said Fenton, slowing down a little so Max could keep up. "It's just that it's not paved."

"Well, if it's a road, I don't see why they don't pave it," Max grumbled.

Fenton sighed. The truth was, he was starting to get a little tired of Max's complaints. The night before, Max had been shocked to discover that the Rumplemayer's house in Morgan didn't have cable TV. "How do they expect you to watch just three channels?" he said. Then there was the way he reacted to the Chinese restaurant that Fenton's father took them to in Fairpoint. "This isn't very authentic; they don't even have chopsticks on the table."

In fact, so far Max didn't seem to appreciate Morgan much at all. He had spent most of that second day at school talking about how things were better at Hibbs. How the teachers at Hibbs were nicer, how Hibbs was more fun because the students got to choose which classes they wanted to take, how the Hibbs library was better because the books were catalogued on computer. Max didn't have one good word to say about Morgan Elementary. It got so bad that Fenton actually felt relieved when the final bell rang for the day.

But now they were on their way to Sleeping Bear, Fenton reminded himself. Now Max would finally get a chance to see the dig site Fenton had told him so much about.

That is, if they ever made it up the mountain. Max was panting pretty heavily now, and Fenton could see little drops of sweat running down his face. His knuckles were white where he was gripping the handlebars, and he was pedaling more slowly than ever.

"Max, are you doing okay?" asked Fenton.

"Yeah, sure, fine," Max panted, pushing at the pedals.

But Max definitely didn't look okay at all. He began to pedal more and more slowly, so slowly that Fenton had difficulty riding at Max's pace and still keeping his balance. Finally, Max climbed off his bicycle altogether and began to walk.

"You go ahead, Fenton," he said, struggling to push the bike up the incline. "I'll catch up with you soon."

But it didn't look like there was any chance of Max's ever catching up. For a moment, Fenton felt like taking off, leaving Max and his complaints behind. But, after all, Max was a guest, and he didn't know the area. So no matter how much of a pain he was being, Fenton knew he couldn't exactly leave him there like that.

"That's okay, Max," said Fenton, climbing off his bike with a sigh. "Actually," he lied, "I could probably use a little break too."

The boys pushed their bikes the rest of the way up the mountain, with Owen walking alongside them. After what seemed like forever, they arrived at the dig site. Mr. Rumplemayer, Professor Martin, and Charlie were digging at the rock.

"Hi, everyone," said Fenton, laying his bike in the grass nearby.

"Hello there, Fenton," said Charlie. "And howdy do to you, Owen. Well, I guess this must be the famous Max."

"Yeah," said Fenton. "Max, this is Professor Martin and Charlie. They work with my dad out here."

"Hi," Max said, dropping his bike to the ground with a clatter. He looked around. "So, where are all the skeletons and stuff you told me about, Fenton?"

"Well, they're only working on one right now," said Fenton. "You know, the Early Cretaceous dinosaur I told you about. All the other fossils that have been found out here were sent to the museum in New York."

"Oh," said Max, looking a little disappointed. "Right."

"So, Dad, how's it going?" asked Fenton, heading toward the excavation site. "Do you have any more of an idea about what kind of dinosaur it is?"

"Well, yes and no," said his father. "Actually, what we've found so far is a bit confusing."

"Come take a look," said Charlie.

Fenton and Max made their way over to the rock. Owen followed them over and lay down at Max's feet, rolling over and putting his belly in the air.

"Wow," said Fenton, when he saw how much more of the dinosaur had been exposed. Not only was the entire scapula visible, but so was the rest of the arm.

"You see," said Mr. Rumplemayer, "from what we've got here now, my best guess would normally be that this is some kind of large theropod, what we call a carnosaur."

"Cool," said Fenton.

Carnosaurs were bipedal meat-eaters that grew to at least twenty feet long and had large heads and sharp teeth. Allosaurus, ceratosaurus, and dilophosaurus had all been carnosaurs. A carnosaur find could be really exciting, especially if it turned out that there was an entire skeleton buried there.

But then, suddenly, Fenton remembered something. Professor Martin had dated the rock at 115 to 120 million years old, to the early Cretaceous. But there were no known North American carnosaurs at all from that period. In fact, most of them had lived in the Jurassic period, between 135 and 200 million years ago.

"Hey, wait a minute," said Fenton. "How can that be a carnosaur?"

"Exactly," said Fenton's father. "Now you see what our problem is."

"What?" said Max, rubbing Owen's stomach and glancing at the pile of bones embedded in the rock. "I don't get it."

"Well," said Fenton, "these bones were found in rock that's 120 million years old at the most. But the last of the carnosaurs in this area died out 15 million years before that."

"Oh," said Max. He shrugged. "I don't see how you can tell what it is from this stuff anyway. If you ask me, it doesn't even look like a dinosaur."

"What do you mean?" said Fenton. "It's all right there— can't you see it? That's the shoulder bone, and those are the bones of the arm, right below it."

"I guess," said Max, scratching Owen's belly.

Fenton realized that it might be kind of difficult to recognize the dinosaur's parts the way they were, embedded in the rock like that, especially if you weren't used to seeing them this way. But Fenton knew exactly what he was looking at. And it definitely didn't make much sense. What would a dinosaur from the Jurassic have been doing walking around in the Cretaceous? Then he thought of something.

"Hey, Dad," he said, "do you think this might be a new kind of carnosaur? Something that no one ever discovered before? A carnosaur that lived in the Cretaceous?"

"Well, I wouldn't go so far as to say that yet, son," said Mr. Rumplemayer. "Although it's possible, of course."

"Or it could turn out to be some other kind of new dinosaur," said Professor Martin. "Something with a similar arm structure to the carnosaurs, or that was even related to them but lived later."

"Only one way to find out for sure," said Charlie, nodding toward the red tool kit that contained the digging equipment.

"Sure thing," said Fenton excitedly. "Hey, Max, come on. You want to dig with me?"

"Uh, okay," said Max, standing up.

"Now, according to the diagrams I've made, we can expect the dinosaur's neck and head to be somewhere over here," said Mr. Rumplemayer, pointing. "Maybe you boys can start clearing away some of that area and see what you come up with."

"Okay," said Fenton.

He selected two large picks and handed one to Max. Then he showed Max how to dig away at the dirt and rock. While the paleontologists finished uncovering the dinosaur's arm bones, the two boys set to work looking for pieces of the head and neck.

After about fifteen minutes of digging, Max sat back on his heels.

"I don't think there's anything here, Fenton," he said.

Charlie chuckled. "Well, you probably have to give it a little more of a chance than that, Max."

"Yeah," said Fenton. "Like I said, sometimes it takes a while to uncover fossils."

Max sighed and went back to work. But ten minutes later he stopped again.

"I don't think I'm going to do any more, Fenton," he said. "My hands are starting to hurt."

"They'll get used to it soon," said Fenton, still digging away.

"No, really," said Max, putting down his pick. "I think I'm starting to get blisters."

Fenton stopped working and looked at him.

"I really have to be careful of my hands," Max said. "Blisters could really mess up my clarinet playing."

"But Max, you're not going to be playing the clarinet for practically another week," Fenton pointed out.

"Yeah, well, I should still watch out," said Max. "I promised Jane I'd give her a few more recorder lessons before I leave."

Fenton couldn't believe his ears. Was Max actually saying that teaching Willy's sister to play the recorder was more important to him than digging for fossils?

"Are you sure, Max?" he asked. "I mean, you could miss out on being part of a really important discovery."

"Yeah, I think I'll just sit and watch for a while," said Max.

He sat down on a rock, and Owen trotted over and lay down on his back to have his stomach rubbed.

Fenton had to admit he was pretty disappointed. It was starting to seem like he and Max had hardly anything in common at all anymore. Had Max changed, or was it Fenton who was different now? Fenton thought back to when he had first moved to Wyoming. Sure, it had been difficult to get used to certain things, like living in a house instead of an apartment, and going to a new school. But Fenton had tried to keep an open mind—at least, he thought he had. Why couldn't Max do the same? If only Max would at least try to get along in Morgan, thought Fenton. But there was no doubt about it; Max may have been his best friend in New York, but in Wyoming he was starting to seem completely out of place.

8

"Max, aren't you finished with that yet?" asked Fenton as the two of them sat in the second-floor study later that night.

Max leaned closer to the computer screen and typed in a few more commands. "Hang on, Fenton. Just a little longer."

"But Max, you've been at this all night," said Fenton.

"Okay, okay, I know," said Max, squinting at the screen. "I just need a few more minutes."

Fenton sighed. "You've been saying that for two hours already."

Max looked at Fenton. "But this is important; you know that. I'm working on my Enrichment Journal."

"Yeah, right, I know," said Fenton. "But we really have to talk about our costumes. After all, the party's only four days away."

Fenton picked up a pencil from the desk and tossed it in the air. So far Max's visit wasn't exactly going the way he had imagined it would. Fenton looked down at Owen, who was asleep under the desk. Even the dog looked bored.

"I'm going downstairs to get dessert," said Fenton, standing up. "You want some ice cream or something?"

"Hmmm," said Max, looking intently at the computer screen.

Fenton shook his head. Max was definitely off in his own world. He probably wouldn't even realize that Fenton had left the room.

Ten minutes later Fenton came back upstairs with two bowls of chocolate ice cream.

"Okay," he said, putting one of the bowls down next to the computer. "Are you done yet?"

"Yeah, yeah, almost," said Max. He sat back and picked up his ice cream.

"So," said Fenton leaning toward the computer screen a little, "what did you say in your journal about the carnosaur problem?"

"The carnosaur problem?" Max repeated.

"Yeah," said Fenton. "You know, the fact that so far the dinosaur looks like a carnosaur, but that the rock isn't old enough for it to be one."

"Oh," said Max, taking a bite of his ice cream. "You mean that thing out at the dig site."

"Well, of course," said Fenton. "That's what you're doing your Enrichment Journal project on, isn't it?"

Max shook his head. "I don't think so, Fenton. Not anymore."

"What do you mean?" said Fenton. "I thought that was the whole point—to do your journal about the dig site."

"That's what I thought at first too," said Max. "But the dig site's too boring."

"Boring!" Fenton repeated, astonished.

"Yeah," said Max. "Things are just too slow out there. You dig and dig and you don't even come up with anything."

"Well, sure, sometimes," said Fenton. "But it's not always like that. Sometimes it's really exciting. You just have to be patient. You should really give it another chance, Max."

Max shrugged. "I guess I'm just not into the dig site, Fenton."

Fenton had to admit he was kind of hurt. The dig site was just about his favorite place in the whole world.

"Well then, what are you going to do for your project?" he asked.

"I'm not sure yet," said Max. "First I want to do some research on the area at the Cheyenne library."

"Cheyenne?" said Fenton. "But that's sixty miles from here. How are you going to get there?"

Max grinned and patted the top of the computer. "With this."

"What do you mean?" asked Fenton.

"Fenton, you've got a modem," said Max. "Don't you realize how great that is? You can communicate with people and get information from all over the place. I can hook up to the

Cheyenne library right from here. The library's system is down right now, but I plan to contact them first thing tomorrow."

"You mean after school," said Fenton.

Max shook his head. "That's another thing. I don't think I'll be going to school with you anymore."

"What?" said Fenton, shocked. "Why not, Max? I thought that was part of our plan."

Max shrugged. "I just think I could use the time better here in front of the computer working on my journal," he said.

Fenton was starting to get pretty fed up. First Max had said he wasn't interested in the dig site anymore, and now he had announced that he wasn't even going to school with Fenton.

"I can't believe you're actually going to spend your whole Enrichment Period in front of that computer," he said angrily.

"Hey, Fenton, cool it," said Max. "You know I have to work on my project. It's an assignment. Besides, I won't be here all day. In the afternoons I can go over to the Whitefoxes and give Jane her recorder lessons when she gets home from school."

Fenton couldn't believe his ears. "Oh, that's just great, Max," he said.

"What's your problem, Fenton?" said Max.

Fenton felt like he was about to burst.

"What's my problem?" he said loudly. "What's my problem? My problem is the way you've been acting ever since you got here, Max. Like nothing in Morgan is good enough for you—not the dig site, not my school, not my friends!"

71

"Hey, Fenton—" Max began.

Fenton cut him off. "And another thing. I've been trying to get you to help me plan our costumes for the party since yesterday, and you won't even talk to me about it!" He shook his head angrily. "You know, I should just go ahead and plan my costume without you."

"Why don't you do that?" Max shot back. "I told you I didn't care about going to that dumb party anyway!"

"Fine!" Fenton yelled. "If that's the way you feel about it, I will go without you."

With that, he turned and headed up the attic steps to his room.

When he got upstairs, Fenton lay across his bed. He was amazed to think that he and Max had just had such a big fight. Fenton had been looking forward to Max's visit so much, but it just didn't seem to be working out at all.

Fenton stood up from his bed and walked across the room to the tiny window that looked out on the backyard. The moon was shining, and a breeze was blowing the fallen leaves around on the ground.

He supposed he should start thinking about his Halloween costume. After all, Willy and Maggie already knew what they were going to be. He couldn't let the fight with Max get him down. He had to get to work on his costume right away, especially if he wanted to have any chance at all at winning that Ping-Pong table.

Fenton picked up one of his dinosaur books from the shelf below the window and began leafing through it. He opened to a page with a large color drawing of a tyrannosaurus rex.

Now, that would be a fun thing to dress up as for Halloween, he thought, looking at the picture. But it might be kind of hard to come up with a good costume for it, especially with only four days to work on it.

Fenton closed the book and put it back on the shelf. As he did, another book caught his eye. It was called *Keys to the Past: Unlocking the Secrets of the Dinosaurs*, and it was all about the important discoveries that had been made in dinosaur science through the years. It was one of Fenton's favorites.

Fenton opened it up. As soon as he started reading, he felt better. The first chapter of the book told the story of Alfred Wegener, who, back in 1915, suggested the idea that the different continents of Earth had once been joined together—that millions of years ago Europe and Africa had slowly drifted apart from North and South America. People had made fun of Wegener at the time, but now the idea of continental drift was accepted as the truth. Today scientists understood that the surface of Earth was constantly changing, as pieces of its outer crust slowly moved around, separating and coming together, forming trenches and mountain ranges. Sometimes sections of land were shifted to entirely new angles, or even turned completely upside down.

Fenton flipped the pages. The next chapter in the book was about Gideon Mantell, the English doctor who had first identified the teeth of the dinosaur iguanodon back in 1822. Wow, thought Fenton, looking at the drawing of Dr. Mantell in his old-fashioned hat and cape, imagine how it must have felt to have discovered one of the first dinosaurs ever known.

Then Fenton had an idea. Maybe he should be Gideon Mantell for Halloween. Now *that* would be a cool costume. All he would need to find was a hat, a cape, and a doctor's bag.

For the first time in more than a day, Fenton actually felt good about the Halloween party. Now that he had his costume planned, it didn't seem like such a big deal that Max didn't want to go. After all, Fenton could have just as good a time at the party without Max, couldn't he?

9

The following afternoon Fenton decided to ride straight out to the dig site after school. He and Max hadn't really spoken since their fight the night before, and Fenton didn't feel like facing him yet. Max had worked kind of late on the computer, and Fenton had already been in bed when he had come upstairs. Then, that morning, when the T-rex alarm clock went off, Max just lay in the sleeping bag while Fenton got ready for school. Max's eyes were closed, but Fenton definitely got the feeling that Max had been awake.

When Fenton got to the dig site, he found his father and the others working on the rock as usual.

"Hi," said Fenton, climbing off his bike. "How's it going?"

"Oh, hello, son," said Mr. Rumplemayer. "Where's Max?"

"Uh, he decided not to come this time," said Fenton. He didn't feel like telling his father about the fight.

"I guess everyone can use a break now and then," said Professor Martin.

"Gee," said Charlie with a wink, "too bad Max chose today to stay home, though. He's going to miss all the excitement."

"What do you mean?" asked Fenton, hurrying over. "Did

76

you find something else? Do you know what kind of dinosaur it is?"

"Not yet," said his father, "but we do think we may have located the animal's skull."

"Thanks to all that preliminary digging you and Max did yesterday," said Professor Martin.

See, thought Fenton. Max was wrong. The work we were doing yesterday *did* turn out to be important after all.

Fenton's father pointed to a large slab of rock that had been marked off with white chalk. Most of the dirt had been dug away from the rock's edges, and Fenton could see a large oblong skull beginning to take shape.

"Wow," said Fenton. "Can I help work on the head?"

"That's right where we need the extra elbow grease," said Charlie.

Fenton selected a medium-sized pick from the tool kit and set to work with the others. As he scraped away at the rock surrounding the bone of the skull, he began to feel a lot better. Soon he was so involved in what he was doing that he completely forgot about his fight with Max.

As time went by, Fenton and the paleontologists uncovered more and more of the skull. Eventually they had exposed all of the lower jawbone.

"Hmmm," said Fenton's father, surveying the fossil. He turned to Professor Martin. "What do you think?"

Professor Martin shook her head.

"I think that what I think I'm seeing can't really be what I'm seeing," she said.

"I'm having the same problem," said Mr. Rumplemayer.

"It does seem awfully strange," agreed Charlie.

"Huh?" said Fenton. "What's going on?"

"Nothing to be concerned about yet," said his father. "It's just—well, let's just wait and see what happens when we get the rest of this uncovered. Who knows? Perhaps we do have a new dinosaur here after all."

"Cool," said Fenton, digging a little faster.

If this turned out to be a brand-new dinosaur, all of them would get credit for having discovered it. Why, they'd even get to name it!

"All right," said Charlie, pointing to a thin, flat slab of rock covering what would have been the top of the animal's head. "Let's try chipping away at the edges of this piece here. If we get it loose enough, maybe we can pull it off."

"Good idea," said Mr. Rumplemayer. "If it works, we could get a very good view of the rest of the skull."

They set to work, and in a little while, they had loosened the slab of rock.

"Ready?" said Mr. Rumplemayer, grabbing one edge of the rock.

"Okay," said Charlie, taking hold of another side.

"I've got it over here," called Professor Martin from another edge.

"And I've got this part," said Fenton.

"On three," said Charlie as they all prepared to move the slab. "One, two, three!"

They pushed, and the piece of rock fell away, revealing the remainder of the dinosaur's skull.

Fenton leaned over eagerly to look at it. After all, this could be his first glimpse of an entirely unknown dinosaur.

But it wasn't a new dinosaur at all. In fact, it was a dinosaur that Fenton knew very well. One look at the skull told him that.

The problem was, nothing was any clearer now than it had been before. As a matter of fact, from what he could tell, things were more confusing than ever.

10

"Okay, wait a minute, Fen," said Maggie as she, Fenton, and Willy headed across the school yard toward the bike rack the next day after school. "Let me get this straight. Are you saying the dinosaur turned out to be even *older* than everyone thought?"

"That's right," sighed Fenton. "As soon as we got the top of the head uncovered, we saw that the dinosaur was a dilophosaurus."

"But dilophosauruses lived in the Early Jurassic, right?" said Maggie.

"Exactly," said Fenton. "In fact, it's the oldest carnosaur known."

"So, I don't get it," said Willy. "What does it all mean?"

"It means," said Fenton, "that somehow a dinosaur from about *200* million years ago ended up misplaced in rock from *120* million years ago."

"That's 80 million years unaccounted for," said Maggie.

"I know," said Fenton glumly. "And *that* means we're further from the answer than ever."

"That sure is weird, Fen," said Maggie. "And your dad and the others haven't figured out how it happened?"

"No," said Fenton. "It just doesn't make sense."

"Couldn't there just have been a couple of those dinosaurs who were still around then?" asked Willy.

"Eighty million years later?" said Fenton. "Not too likely."

"Then maybe it's not actually a dilophosaurus at all," suggested Maggie. "Maybe it's some other kind of dinosaur."

"Nope," said Fenton. "It's definitely a dilophosaurus. You see, dilophosauruses had this special double-ridged crest on top of their heads."

"Oh, right," said Maggie. "It sort of looks like the two halves of a broken plate, right?"

"Right," said Fenton.

"Well, the whole thing sounds like a pretty big mystery to me," said Maggie.

That was exactly what it sounded like to Fenton, too—a mystery. And it was a mystery he was determined to solve.

Suddenly Willy pointed toward the bike rack.

"Hey, look," he said. "There's Max."

To Fenton's surprise, Willy was right. There, standing by the bike rack, with Willy's mother's bike leaning against his hip, was Max.

"Hi, everyone," said Max. He looked at Fenton and smiled a little sheepishly. "Hi, Fenton."

"Hi," said Fenton, feeling a little funny. He and Max had been pretty much avoiding each other since the argument.

"Hey, I thought you were sort of staying inside these days," said Maggie. "You know, to work on that project of yours."

"Yeah," said Willy. "Fenton said that's why you weren't coming to school anymore."

Max shrugged. "I guess I figured I could use a break. I thought maybe we could all go check out that place Fenton told me about. You know, the rock museum or whatever it is."

"Mrs. Wadsworth's?" said Fenton. "Sure, I guess so."

"Good idea," said Maggie, pulling her bike out of the rack.

"Yeah," said Willy. "We haven't been there in a while. Maybe she's got some new stuff."

They climbed on their bikes and set off together, with Willy and Maggie in the lead.

"Hey," said Max, turning to Fenton. "Sorry about all that stuff the other night."

"Yeah," said Fenton, pushing down on his pedals. "Me too."

Ten minutes later they rode into the parking lot of the WADSWORTH MUSEUM OF ROCKS & OTHER NATURAL CURIOS and rested their bikes against the fence. As they walked inside, Fenton felt better than he had in days. Not only had he and Max made up, but there was something about Mrs. Wadsworth's place, with its collection of rocks, bones, feathers, and other artifacts, that always cheered him up. It was almost enough to make him forget about the problem out at the dig site.

Even Max seemed impressed by the place. After the way things had gone at the beginning of the week, Fenton hadn't expected him to think much of Mrs. Wadsworth's. But Max seemed in a much better mood. In fact, as soon as they walked into the little red building, he began examining the items set out on the shelves and tabletops with interest.

"Hey, look," he said, pointing to a hollow wooden tube about three feet long that was leaning against a wall. "This looks like some kind of instrument."

Fenton peered at the carefully lettered label on the wall nearby. "It says here that this is a replica of an Australian instrument made from a branch that's been hollowed out by termites."

Max put the end of the instrument to his mouth, and a deep, vibrating sound, almost like a foghorn, came out.

"Wow," he said. "That's great. Hey, I bet Jane would really get a kick out of it. She'd think it was a giant recorder or something."

"Are you really teaching her to play the recorder?" asked Maggie, peering down to examine a rock on a shelf.

"Sure," said Max. "She's a pretty good student, too."

"Yeah," laughed Willy. "I bet."

"No, really," said Max. "She's working hard at it." He blew into the instrument again. "Wow, this is great."

Just then Mrs. Wadsworth came out of the room in the back, where she lived.

"I *thought* I heard someone playing my didgeridoo," she said, peering over her half-moon spectacles.

"Oops, sorry," said Max, putting the instrument back.

"No, no, by all means, go ahead," said Mrs. Wadsworth. "That's what it's for, you know."

"Hi, Mrs. Wadsworth," said Fenton. "This is my friend Max from New York."

"Welcome, Max," she said. "Any friend of Fenton's is a friend of mine. Hello, Maggie and Willy."

"What did you say this thing was called?" asked Max, pointing to the instrument.

"A didgeridoo," said Mrs. Wadsworth. "The real ones are Australian, but this is an exact replica. I traded for it. Just yesterday, in fact, from a gentleman who was passing through. Well, the minute I saw it I just had to have it, so I offered him two stuffed jackrabbits."

"Wow, Mrs. Wadsworth," said Fenton. "I didn't realize you traded with people for stuff."

"Well, sure," she said. "Whenever I can. Otherwise I'd never be able to get certain items."

That makes sense, thought Fenton. I guess there aren't too many didgeridoos in Morgan.

"Actually, I'd like to trade more often than I do," she went on. "But it's hard to get in touch with other people who are

willing to make exchanges. And goodness knows folks don't pass through here too often."

"You should set up an electronic bulletin board for it," said Max.

"What kind of bulletin board?" asked Mrs. Wadsworth, looking interested.

"Well, it's not *really* a bulletin board," Max explained. "I mean, not the kind you put on a real wall or anything. It's something you do on a computer."

"A computer," Mrs. Wadsworth repeated. "How fascinating."

"Yeah," said Max enthusiastically. "You can do all kinds of stuff with computers, especially if you've got a modem so you can communicate with other computers."

"I get it," said Maggie. "Mrs. Wadsworth could put announcements about things she wants to trade and things she's looking for onto the electronic bulletin board."

"Right," said Max. "And other people who want to trade could use it too."

"How marvelous that sounds," said Mrs. Wadsworth.

"Hold on a sec," said Willy. "Wouldn't Mrs. Wadsworth need to have a computer?"

"Oh," said Max. "I guess you don't have one, huh?"

"No," said Mrs. Wadsworth, shaking her head.

"Too bad," said Max. Then he brightened. "But maybe Fenton could do it for you on his computer. You could write out the announcements you wanted, and he could put them onto the bulletin board for you."

"Sure," volunteered Fenton. "But can my computer do that?"

"Of course," said Max. "Like I told you, Fenton, you have a modem. That means you can do all kinds of things. Why, just this morning I used the computer to look at a photograph that was over a hundred years old on file at the Cheyenne library."

"You did?" said Fenton. "A photograph of what?"

"Oh, um, just something I needed to look at for my Enrichment Journal," Max said quickly. "But that's not the point. The point is, if you have a modem you can do all kinds of stuff."

"Well," said Mrs. Wadsworth. "It certainly all sounds wonderful. It's amazing what can be done these days."

"It's great," said Max. "Just wait and see. I'll show Fenton how to set it up before I leave."

"Why, thank you, Max," said Mrs. Wadsworth. "That's very kind of you. I owe you a favor."

"No problem, Mrs. Wadsworth," said Max. "I love doing this kind of stuff."

Later that evening, as Fenton and Max were helping Mr. Rumplemayer with the dinner dishes, the telephone rang. Mr. Rumplemayer put down the sponge he was using to wipe the counters and picked up the receiver.

"Hello?" he said. "Oh, hello, Willy. Yes, he's right here, just a moment." He held out the telephone. "Fenton, it's for you."

"Okay," said Fenton. "Just a sec."

He ran the last of the plates under the faucet and handed it to Max to dry. Then he took the phone from his father.

"Hi, Willy," he said. "What's up?"

"Hi," said Willy. "Listen, how'd you like to go to the Fairpoint mall tomorrow after school?"

"Sure, I guess," said Fenton. "What for?"

"Well," said Willy, "there's this big stationery store there called Card Castle, and they sell costume stuff, too. I thought if you still needed to get some stuff for your Dr. Mantell outfit, you might want to check it out."

"Great," said Fenton. "How are we getting there?"

"My dad said he'd take us," said Willy. "He has to get some electrical stuff for the party."

"Okay," said Fenton. "Sounds good. I'll call Maggie."

"I just talked to her," said Willy. "She wants to come too. Oh, and bring Max, too, if you want."

"Yeah, I don't know," said Fenton, looking around the kitchen. Max and his father had finished cleaning up and left the room. "I don't think Max is really into the costume party."

"Okay, whatever," said Willy. "He could always check out that N-Force game at the mall while we're shopping."

"Yeah, I think he's pretty busy here with his project," said Fenton. "But thanks anyway, Willy."

"Okay, Fenton," said Willy. "See you tomorrow."

Fenton hung up the phone and thought a moment. What *about* Max? It was true that Max had said he wasn't interested in the party, but maybe Fenton should check and make sure anyway.

Fenton made his way up the stairs to the second floor. As he walked into the study, he could hear Max clicking the computer's mouse.

"Hi," Fenton said, swinging around the corner into the room.

Max looked up from the computer in surprise.

"Fenton!" he said. "What are you doing here? I mean, I thought you were on the phone or something."

"I was," said Fenton, walking over toward the computer. "But I'm off now."

"Oh," said Max, suddenly clicking the mouse very rapidly. "Hang on, let me just—" He typed a few quick commands onto the keyboard.

"What are you doing?" Fenton asked, leaning over Max's shoulder. "Working on your Enrichment Journal again?"

"Uh, yeah, that's right," said Max.

But when Fenton looked at the screen, it was blank.

"I don't see anything," he said.

"Well, uh, that's because, um, because I'm just about to start a new entry," said Max quickly. He pressed a few keys. "See?"

Fenton looked at the screen. It said:

"I thought you said you were designing the program to put in the date for you automatically," said Fenton.

"Oh, that's right," said Max. "I guess I forgot."

It was awfully strange for Max to forget anything having to do with a computer, thought Fenton. Especially something he himself had designed. As a matter of fact, Max had been acting a little odd ever since Fenton had come into the room.

"What is it you're writing about for your project, anyway?" asked Fenton.

"Oh, nothing really," said Max. "Just sort of, you know, researching the area, like I told you."

"Yeah, but exactly what are you researching?" asked Fenton, getting more curious.

"Nothing too interesting," said Max. "You know, just a few facts about Morgan."

"Oh yeah?" said Fenton. "That sounds kind of neat. What kind of facts have you found out?"

"Nothing much," said Max. "I mean, I can't remember." He reached behind the computer and switched it off. "Well, I guess I'll stop for the night."

Now there was definitely something strange about *that*. Fenton didn't think he could remember Max *ever* having just turned off a computer like that.

Just then Owen trotted in. He walked over to Max and lay

down on the floor, rolling onto his back. Max bent down to pet his belly.

"Listen, Max," said Fenton, pulling up a chair. "I want to ask you something."

"Sure," said Max. "Shoot."

"It's about the Halloween party at the firehouse," said Fenton.

Max looked a little guilty. "Gee, I'm sorry I said all that nasty stuff about the party, Fenton."

"That's okay," said Fenton. "But the thing is, I went ahead and planned a costume without you."

"So?" said Max.

"So, are you still sure you don't want to go?" asked Fenton. "Because if you do, Maggie and Willy and I were thinking of heading over to a costume shop in Fairpoint tomorrow. You could probably find something to wear there."

Max smiled for a moment, then shook his head. "That's okay, Fenton. I really have too much work to do here anyway."

"Are you sure?" said Fenton.

"Yeah, don't worry about me," said Max. "I really have a lot of last-minute stuff to do on my project. I'll probably just spend all my free time right here working. I won't even have time for the party." He paused. "And if I did find the time to go, I'm sure I could always come up with some kind of costume on my own."

"Well, okay," said Fenton. "If you say so."

"Yeah," said Max. "I'm sure. You go ahead and have a good time."

Fenton had to admit he was still a little disappointed. But after all, he thought, I can't *force* Max do go to the party if he doesn't want to, not if he really is happier working here in front of the computer.

11

"Hey, look at this!" said Willy, holding up a bright orange mask. "This would be perfect for my costume." He put the mask up to his face. "I am Eon, master of time," he said in a deep voice.

It was Friday, the day before the Halloween party, and Fenton, Willy, and Maggie were shopping at Card Castle, the big stationery and costume store at the Fairpoint mall.

"What do you think of these?" asked Fenton, putting on a pair of wire-rimmed spectacles.

"Good," said Maggie. "They make you look really old-fashioned."

"And smart," added Willy.

"Willy, people who wear glasses aren't any smarter that people who don't," said Maggie.

"What about Max?" said Willy. "He wears glasses, and he's a computer genius, right?"

"Max may be a computer genius, but if you ask me, he doesn't seem too smart about certain other things," said Maggie. "Sorry, Fen, I know he's your friend."

"No, it's okay," said Fenton. "Max hasn't exactly been that nice to you guys. I think maybe it's been kind of hard for him to get used to Morgan."

"He did seem a lot happier when we saw him yesterday," said Maggie.

"That's true," said Fenton.

"Why didn't he want to come with us?" asked Willy.

"I don't know," said Fenton, shaking his head. "He's still acting kind of funny. The only thing he seems to want to do is work on the computer, but he won't even tell me what it is he's working on."

"Well, then it's his loss," said Maggie. She looked at Fenton. "You know, Willy's right, though. I don't know why, but those glasses do make you look kind of smart."

"Well, Dr. Mantell was smart," said Fenton. "He discovered the iguanodon."

"But some people say it was actually Mrs. Mantell who found the dinosaur teeth," said Maggie. "I read about it in a book."

"Boy, Maggie," said Willy. "How many books have you read, a million?"

Maggie shrugged. "Maybe," she said with a grin. "Now, let's

find the wigs, you guys, so I can pick out something for my Hatshepsut outfit."

Twenty minutes later, they were done with their shopping. Fenton had bought the glasses, along with a black hat, a doctor's black bag with buckles, a black cape, and a fake moustache. He had even managed to find a necklace of big plastic animal teeth that was supposed to be part of a caveman costume. He planned to cut off the teeth and put them all in a jar to carry with him to the party. They could represent the iguanodon teeth.

Now that his costume was set, Fenton was looking forward to the Halloween party more than ever. Who knew, maybe his Dr. Mantell costume would even win first prize. Having a Ping-Pong table would be great. He and Maggie and Willy could play all the time.

When Mr. Whitefox dropped him back off in front of his house later that afternoon, Fenton was surprised to see the green pickup truck in the driveway. It was unusual for his father to be home from the dig site before dark, especially when the team was in the middle of excavating a dinosaur.

Fenton found his father sitting on the living-room couch, a sheet of paper in his hand.

"Hi, Dad. What are you doing here?" he asked.

"Oh, hello, son," said Mr. Rumplemayer, looking up from the paper. "Things weren't going all that well out at the dig site, so we decided to stop a little early."

"I guess that means you still haven't managed to figure out what that dilophosaurus was doing in the Cretaceous rock," said Fenton, sitting down next to his father.

"That's right," said Mr. Rumplemayer. He shook his head. "I just can't understand it. And now we have another problem."

"What's that?" asked Fenton.

"Finding the rest of the dinosaur," said his father.

"What do you mean?" said Fenton.

"We can't seem to locate a trace of anything below the dilophosaurus's shoulders," said Mr. Rumplemayer. "It's odd, because the fossil find above the shoulder area is so complete."

"That's weird," said Fenton.

"I know," said his father. "The rest of the body just doesn't seem to be where it should be. Or anywhere, for that matter." He sighed. "I've been studying this diagram since I got home, but I just can't seem to figure out where we went wrong." He put the paper down on the couch. "Well, I don't seem to be getting anywhere with this. I'll tell you what. Why don't we drive into town and pick up some steaks? Then, when Max gets back, maybe we can have a barbecue. I know it's getting a little chilly out for that, but—"

"When Max gets home?" Fenton repeated, cutting him off. "What do you mean? Isn't he upstairs?"

"Why, no," said Mr. Rumplemayer. "I thought you knew. He left a note in the kitchen saying he was going to the Whitefoxes'."

"Oh," said Fenton. "He's been giving Willy's little sister recorder lessons."

"That's nice," said Mr. Rumplemayer.

"Yeah, I guess," said Fenton.

But he couldn't help thinking, if Max was so busy with last-minute work on his Enrichment Journal, how had he found the time to go over to the Whitefoxes' and help Jane?

12

"Thanks a lot for giving me a ride, you guys," said Willy, squeezing into the backseat of the red convertible with Maggie, Fenton, and Owen. "Hey, I didn't know Owen was coming."

"He wasn't," said Fenton. "But at the last moment he jumped into the car and wouldn't get out."

"Maybe he'll win a prize for his dog costume," said Willy, laughing.

It was Saturday evening, the night of the Halloween party, and Maggie's sister, Lila, and Lila's boyfriend, Rob, were driving them into town for the party.

"Ugh!" said Lila as the car pulled out of Willy's driveway. "Can you tell that mutt to stop breathing down my neck, please? It's disgusting."

"Sorry," said Fenton, readjusting Owen on his lap.

"Rob, could you slow down a little?" said Maggie.

"Oh, Maggie, please," said Lila. "We're already going about ten miles an hour."

"But the wind is messing up my wig," Maggie complained. "Sisters," she said under her breath.

"Tell me about it," agreed Willy. "You should have seen

mine tonight. Jane refused to put on her costume until I left, and she wouldn't tell me anything about it. It's some big secret or something. She's even making my mom drive her separately to the party."

"That's kind of cute," said Fenton.

"Kind of dumb is more like it," said Willy. "I mean, does she really think I won't recognize her anyway the second she gets there?"

"Hey, speaking of costumes," said Maggie. "Why aren't you and Rob dressed up, Lila?"

"Please," said Lila. "I think we're a little old for that kind of stuff. We're only going to the party to hear the band. Rob's got some friends in it from school."

I hope I never get too old to get dressed up for Halloween, thought Fenton. It's definitely one of the best holidays there is.

Ten minutes later they pulled up in front of the firehouse. The two fire trucks were parked outside, and there were lighted jack-o'-lanterns sitting on them. A big green tent was glowing with light in front of the red-brick building, and Fenton could hear music playing somewhere inside. The outside of the tent and of the firehouse itself had been decorated with orange and black crepe paper, and a big banner had been strung between two trees:

Happy Halloween!
Happy 125th Anniversary, Morgan!

"Wow," said Maggie, climbing out of the car, "this looks even better than last year!"

"My dad and the others were here all day setting things up," said Willy. "Come on, let's go inside."

As Fenton followed Maggie and Willy toward the tent with Owen, he couldn't help thinking how great they all looked in their costumes. In her white tunic and black wig, and with her eyes made up like an ancient Egyptian's, Maggie was almost unrecognizable. And Willy looked practically like a real super-hero, with his orange cape and tights and the little silver wings fastened to his ankles. Fenton was pleased with his costume too. He felt just like Gideon Mantell in his black hat and cape, and the jar of plastic teeth was the perfect touch.

They walked into the tent, and Fenton looked around. Several small wooden stalls with games had been set up on the left side of the tent, and a bunch of kids in costumes were gathered around them. Opposite the stalls were two long tables, covered with plates of food and big bowls of Halloween candy. Through the big open door that led into the firehouse itself, he could see the band playing on a high wooden platform. Everywhere there were orange and black streamers and balloons.

"Wow," said Maggie. "Your friend Max is really missing out."

"I know," said Fenton, watching as Owen bounded off into the crowd. "I tried one last time to get him to come, but he was working on the computer as usual." He shook his head. "He's been in front of that computer all week! Except yesterday, that is, when he went over to your place, Willy."

"Oh, yeah," said Willy. "My mom did say he had been there, helping Jane with her recorder or something."

"Didn't you see him yourself?" asked Fenton. "Wasn't he there when we got back from buying the costume stuff in Fairpoint?"

"No," said Willy. "From what my mother said, I think he came much earlier in the afternoon."

"That's weird," said Fenton.

"What?" asked Maggie.

"Well, Max didn't get home until about five-thirty or six o'clock yesterday," said Fenton. "When he came in, he said he'd gone over to Willy's to help Jane, but if he left there earlier in the afternoon, where did he go after that?"

"Who knows?" said Maggie. "Hey, look at Chief Gonzalez!"

The fire chief was dressed in his regular uniform and hat, but his face was made up with orange and black greasepaint to look like a jack-o'-lantern.

"That's pretty funny," said Fenton. "Do you think he's going to enter the contest?"

"He can't," said Willy. "He's one of the judges. It's him and his wife and two other firefighters."

Maggie lowered her voice. "So, what do you think of the other costumes, guys? Do we have a good chance at the Ping-Pong table, or what?"

"I don't know," said Willy. "Some of these other costumes look pretty good."

"Yeah, but they're all so predictable," said Maggie. "You know, skeletons, vampires, witches. And there must be at least a dozen ghosts here."

Fenton looked around. It was true; most of the other costumes were pretty typical for Halloween.

"I guess you're right," he said. "I mean, if being original really does count, then there's probably a good chance that one of us will win."

"And if one of us wins, we all win," Willy pointed out. "'Cause you can't exactly play Ping-Pong alone, you know."

"That's true," said Maggie. "Hey, what do you say we go get some food—I'm starved."

When they got to the food table, they found Owen there, begging scraps from people's plates.

"What a cute dog," said Lisa Levine, who was dressed as a giant carrot. "Is he yours?"

"Yeah," said Fenton. He slipped the jar of teeth into his doctor bag and grabbed hold of Owen's collar. "I guess I'd better hold on to him so he doesn't eat too much junk."

"Hey," said Lisa. "Neat costumes. What are you guys supposed to be?"

"I'm Eon. He's a superhero who can travel through time," said Willy.

"I'm Gideon Mantell," said Fenton, "the English doctor

who discovered the dinosaur iguanodon."

"And I'm Hatshepsut," said Maggie. "She was Egypt's only female pharaoh."

"Oh," said Lisa. "I'm a carrot." She shrugged inside her orange costume. "It's not that exciting, but it was the most original thing I could think of."

"It's good," said Fenton. "I mean, it's definitely original. You're the only carrot I've seen here."

"Yeah," said Lisa. "I thought it might be a good way to make the judges notice me. But I guess it looks like Buster has the contest sewn up."

"What are you talking about?" said Fenton.

"Oh, you mean you haven't seen his costume yet?" asked Lisa.

"No," said Maggie. "What's he wearing?"

"Just look," said Lisa, pointing across the room.

There, standing by one of the game booths with his back to them, pitching baseballs at a stack of empty cans, was Buster. He had on a jean jacket, jeans, sneakers, and a cowboy hat.

"I don't get it," said Fenton. "What's he supposed to be?"

"Wait till he's finished," said Lisa. "You'll see."

Buster pitched his last ball, missing the cans entirely.

"Oh, man," he said, turning away in disgust. "This game's fixed."

He leaned down and picked up a three-foot-wide, irregular rectangle of thin plywood from the ground.

"Oh my gosh," said Maggie as Buster turned around. "I get it. That's Wyoming."

In fact, the shape of the wood did look a lot like the state of Wyoming did on the map. Scrawled in red marker near the bottom of the rectangle was a dot labeled MORGAN, and taped across the top of the wood was a small, multicolored Happy Birthday banner. Buster reached into his jean jacket pocket, pulled out a party noisemaker, put it to his lips, and blew hard.

"Happy birthday, Morgan!" he yelled, looking around and grinning.

"So?" said Willy. "It's not really that great a costume. I mean, I bet he didn't work on it very hard. His uncle owns the lumberyard; he probably just picked up that piece of wood there and wrote Morgan on it with a marker."

"Yeah," said Fenton. "It's not like Wyoming is a complicated shape or anything."

"Yeah, but remember, it's Morgan's hundred and twenty-fifth anniversary this year," said Maggie glumly. "So I bet the judges are really going to go for it."

"I guess it *is* a pretty original idea," admitted Fenton.

"Yeah," said Lisa. "The way I figure it, that Ping-Pong table is already Buster's."

Just then the music stopped playing, and Chief Gonzalez's voice came over the microphone.

"All right, everyone," he boomed. "Quiet down, please. I'd like to welcome you all to the Halloween party this year—a very special year, I might add, since we are also celebrating the one hundred and twenty-fifth anniversary of the founding of Morgan."

"Yeah!" yelled Buster. He blew his noisemaker. "Happy birthday, Morgan!"

Chief Gonzalez smiled.

"Forget it," said Willy. "We're sunk. There's no way we can win now."

Chief Gonzalez cleared his throat. "I'd like to ask everyone who is participating in the contest to line up against this wall so the judges can take a look at you," he said, pointing to his left.

"Oh, well," said Maggie as they joined the line of kids against the wall. "It was still fun dressing up, right, Fen?"

But Fenton didn't answer her. He was busy looking at someone. Someone very tall, in a big hat with a feather and a long coat, who had just come into the firehouse and joined the end of the line.

13

"Who is *that*?" asked Fenton, pointing to the figure at the end of the line.

Maggie squinted. "Beats me."

"Oh, wow!" said Willy. "Don't you guys get it?"

"What do you mean?" asked Fenton. "Get what? Do you know that person?"

"I know who it's *supposed* to be," said Willy, grinning. "And so do you, I bet."

Fenton looked back at the figure. Whoever was inside the costume must be over six feet tall. The big hat with the feather in its brim was tilted to cover the face; all that was visible was a long, scraggly mop of a beard streaked with fluffy white stuff. Tufts of the cottony white stuff covered the hat and coat as well, and some kind of animal skin was slung over the person's back, like a shawl or a cape.

"It's Mighty Morgan!" said Fenton and Maggie together.

"That's right," said Willy. "See? That's his beard, and all that white stuff on him is the snow from the avalanche. And that thing on his back is a bearskin."

"What a great idea for a costume," said Maggie.

"I know," said Willy. "I wish I'd thought of it."

"That ought to give Buster some competition," said Fenton. "Except . . . can grownups enter the contest?"

"That's no grownup," said Maggie. "The shoulders are way too narrow. I bet it's a kid on stilts or something."

"Cool," said Fenton. "What an amazing costume."

"Hey," said Willy, "here come the judges."

Fenton pulled the jar of teeth out of his doctor bag and adjusted his moustache and spectacles.

"Sit," he commanded Owen.

Chief Gonzalez and the other three judges made their way down the line.

"Stay," he said to Owen. "Don't make any trouble."

"Very nice," said Mrs. Gonzalez, looking from Fenton's doctor bag to Owen and making a note on her clipboard. "A veterinarian." Then she saw the jar of teeth in Fenton's other hand and wrinkled up her forehead in confusion. "Or a veterinary dentist?"

Fenton was just about to correct her when Chief Gonzalez announced that it was time for the judges to make their decisions.

"I bet Mighty Morgan wins," whispered Willy as the four judges gathered in a corner of the room.

Chief Gonzalez climbed onto the stage and tapped the microphone.

"All right, the judges have decided," he said. "There are many fine costumes here tonight, but I must say, I think the decision we've reached is most appropriate, given the fact that our town is celebrating its one hundred and twenty-fifth anniversary this year."

Buster took a step forward from the line.

"Look," said Maggie, nudging Fenton. "Buster's pretty sure of himself, huh?"

"And the winning costume is . . ." Chief Gonzalez paused and looked around the room. "Mighty Morgan!"

"Told you," said Willy as the applause began.

"Hey, at least Buster didn't get it," said Maggie.

"Yeah," said Fenton. "Besides, Mighty Morgan is a good costume. Whoever it is deserves to win the Ping-Pong table."

"I'd really like to know who *is* under there," said Maggie, frowning.

Just then Owen jumped up and bounded down the line of kids toward the person in the Mighty Morgan costume.

"Oh, no!" cried Fenton. "Come back!"

Owen sniffed Mighty Morgan's ankles, his tail wagging wildly.

"Come here!" Fenton hissed.

Owen barked once and rolled over onto his back, belly up.

"Hey, wait a minute," said Fenton. "Owen does that for only one person. I know who that is. . . ."

Mighty Morgan looked down from under his hat and began to giggle in a high-pitched voice.

"Me too!" said Willy. "I'd recognize that laugh anywhere!"

"It's Max!" said Fenton.

"It's Jane!" said Willy at the same time.

14

"All right," said Fenton as he, Max, Maggie, Willy, and Jane sat outside the tent, eating Halloween candy. "Start at the beginning, Max."

"Well," said Max, "I was working on my Enrichment Journal and I got to thinking about that story about the founding of Morgan."

"Right," said Willy. "Mighty Morgan and the avalanche."

"That's why Max put the cotton on the costume," Jane chimed in. "To look like the snow from the lavalance."

"Avalanche, Jane," corrected Willy.

"Right," said Jane. "That's what I said."

"Anyway," said Max. "I decided to do a little research on this character Mighty Morgan, just to see if there was any truth at all to the story. So I used the computer's modem to look up some stuff at the Cheyenne library."

"So *that* was what you were researching all that time on the computer," said Fenton.

"Yeah," said Max. "I looked up this old diary of some settler who lived in the area. And according to what he wrote, there was actually a really big blizzard in this area in November exactly a hundred and twenty-five years ago."

"I told you," said Willy.

"I know," said Max. "But I really wanted to find out for myself."

"And so that convinced you that the story was true?" said Maggie.

"That and one other thing," said Max. "As I was searching through old records, I actually found a picture of Mighty Morgan himself."

"The old picture you said you had looked at on the computer!" said Fenton.

"Right," said Max.

"So, what did he look like?" asked Maggie.

"I know," said Willy. "He was seven feet tall, and he had a beard that was two feet long, right?"

"Actually, that's pretty close," said Max. "The picture was really dark, so it was kind of hard to see, but he did have a pretty long beard, and he was definitely very tall. And strong looking, too." He glanced at Willy. "Maybe even strong enough to wrestle a bear with his bare hands."

"I told you! I told you!" said Willy excitedly.

"And there was something else, too," said Max. "There was a name written on the bottom of the photograph."

"A name?" Maggie repeated.

"Yeah," said Max. "It was Mighty Morgan's name—his real name."

"What do you mean?" asked Willy.

"Well," said Max. "It turns out that Mighty Morgan was just a nickname. His real name was *Max* Morgan."

"You're kidding," said Fenton.

Max shook his head. "Pretty amazing, huh? And you know, if I hadn't looked all that stuff up in the library, I would have just gone on thinking the whole story was a fake."

"But I *told* you it was all true," said Willy.

"Yeah, I know," said Max. "And I guess it was wrong of me not to even give the story a chance. Actually, the more I thought about it, the more I began to realize that maybe I hadn't given *Morgan* much of a chance, either. So then I got to thinking, maybe I should surprise everyone by being Mighty Max Morgan for Halloween."

"And I got to sit on his shoulders to make him tall enough," Jane put in.

"So where'd you get all the stuff for the costume?" asked Maggie.

"My mom gave us the coat and the hat," said Jane.

"That's right," said Max. "And I bought the cotton balls and the mop for the beard down at the Morgan Market yesterday afternoon."

"So that's where you went when you left Willy's," said Fenton.

"Hold on a minute, though," said Maggie. "What about the bearskin? Last time I looked, they didn't have any bearskins at the Morgan Market."

"But there is one place in Morgan that has that kind of stuff," said Max. "You guys should know; you took me there the first time."

"Mrs. Wadsworth's!" said Fenton.

"Remember she said she owed me a favor?" said Max. "Well, I decided to take her up on it and borrow this bearskin."

"Definitely a very cool costume," said Willy appreciatively.

"I almost wish I could take it back to New York and wear it to school for my Enrichment Journal presentation," said Max.

"But if you take the costume," said Jane giggling, "then you have to take me, too, 'cause I'm part of it."

"I bet you'd nab an A for sure if you showed up at school looking like that," said Maggie.

"Actually, we don't have grades at my school," said Max.

"Wow," said Willy. "No grades? That's great!"

"In a way," said Max. "Except sometimes, when you know you've done something really good. Then it kind of stinks."

"I guess it's sort of a good thing you decided not to do your journal on the dig site, after all," said Fenton. "The way things are going out there, all you would have ended up with is a bunch of questions and no answers."

Maggie shook her head. "It sure is weird, Fen. I mean, there must be some sort of logical explanation for how that dilophosaurus got buried in that Cretaceous rock."

"That's what I thought, too," said Fenton. "But it just doesn't make sense. Unless you believe in time travel." He looked at Willy. "No offence, Eon."

"Hey, you know what I just thought of?" said Willy. "In a way, I'm not the only one here dressed as a time traveler."

"What do you mean?" asked Max.

"Just look at our costumes," said Willy. "Maggie's from ancient Egypt, and Fenton's from a long time ago, too, right?"

"The 1800's," said Fenton, nodding.

"And Mighty Morgan's from a hundred and twenty-five years ago," said Willy. "So it's almost like we all traveled through to today."

"Now *that's* what I call a time zone difference," joked Max. They all laughed.

"Hey, Max," said Jane. "Can I ask you a question now?"

"Sure," he answered. "Go ahead."

"What exactly *is* a lavalance?" she asked.

"Avalanche," said Willy, sighing.

"An avalanche is when a whole bunch of snow falls down a mountainside and buries everything at the bottom," said Max.

"Actually," said Fenton, "an avalanche doesn't even have to be snow, although most people think of it that way. An avalanche is any kind of big slide down a mountain. It could be snow, or rock, or even a mudslide—"

Suddenly, Fenton stopped.

"Or even a *mudslide!*" he said again.

"Fen?" said Maggie. "Are you okay?"

"Am I ever!" said Fenton, beaming. He looked around at the others. "You guys, I think I may have just solved the mystery of the dilophosaurus!"

15

"I play winner!" said Maggie, tossing a Ping-Pong ball in the air and catching it.

"What about me?" whined Jane. "It's half my Ping-Pong table, you know."

"Yeah, but Max gave his half to *us*," said Willy, hitting the ball across the table to Fenton.

"I'll play with you later, Jane," said Fenton, returning the ball to Willy.

"Okay, Fenkon," she said. She picked up her recorder and carefully began to play a simple tune.

It was a week after the party, and the four of them were down in the Whitefoxes' basement, playing with the new Ping-Pong table.

"That's twenty-one," said Maggie as Willy missed his shot. "Hand over that paddle." Willy passed Maggie the Ping-Pong paddle and leaned against the wall.

"So, Fen," said Maggie, serving Fenton the ball, "tell me

about this business with the dilophosaurus. How exactly did it end up in the Cretaceous rock?"

"Well," said Fenton, reaching for a shot, "it seems like the dinosaur was first fossilized back in the early Jurassic, when it lived and died."

"Okay," said Maggie. "Makes sense so far."

"Then, sometime during the Cretaceous, the piece of earth that was around its head, neck, and arms kind of broke away and shifted. It probably ended up being pushed up higher, maybe by the formation of a mountainside."

"Wow, that's weird," said Willy.

"Actually it happens a lot," said Fenton. "That's one reason why so many fossil finds are incomplete.

"Then the dirt covering the part of the dinosaur that was high up on the mountain was worn away a little by the weather, and the dinosaur's head and arms began to be exposed."

"But," said Maggie, laughing, "since there weren't any paleontologists back in the Cretaceous, no one dug it out and put it in a museum, so it just stayed there."

"Then why didn't the bones disintegrate?" asked Willy. "I thought you said bones had to be covered to be preserved."

"Yeah," said Maggie. "And where did the Cretaceous rock come from?"

"The bones must have been buried again pretty quickly," said Fenton, "probably by some kind of mud avalanche."

"And Mighty Morgan wasn't around back then to dig them

out," said Willy. "So the dirt that covered them over preserved them until now."

"Right," said Fenton. "And in the dirt were teeth from some Cretaceous mammals."

"Which is how you end up with a Jurassic dinosaur covered with Cretaceous rock," said Maggie as Fenton missed his shot. "Okay, that's twenty-one again. Your turn, Willy."

Fenton passed Willy his Ping-Pong paddle.

"Here you go, Willy," said Maggie, tossing him the ball. "Challenger serves first."

Fenton watched as she returned Willy's serve and he missed his shot.

"Jane!" said Willy in an annoyed voice. "Can you please stop playing that thing? You made me miss the ball. What is that dumb song anyway?"

Jane took the recorder out of her mouth.

"It's 'Hot Cross Buns,'" she said. "Max taught it to me. And it's not a dumb song."

"It is so," said Willy.

"Don't be mean to me," said Jane. "Or I won't let you play with my half of the Ping-Pong table anymore."

She picked up her recorder and began to play again. Willy sighed.

"So," said Maggie, returning Willy's shot, "how is Max, anyway, Fen?"

"Good," said Fenton. "He said his Enrichment Journal

went over really well at school. Everybody really liked the story of Mighty Morgan."

"I guess his teacher must have been pretty impressed by that fancy computer stuff he did, too," said Maggie. "You know, the way he said he was going to get it to play music and everything."

"Actually," said Fenton, "Max didn't even end up using the computer for his presentation."

"You're kidding," said Maggie.

"Why not?" asked Willy.

"He decided that the story of Mighty Morgan would be more convincing if he did it in a more authentic way," said Fenton. "So he wrote the whole thing out on this really worn-looking, yellowed paper to make it look like it might actually be a hundred and twenty-five years old."

"I get it," said Willy.

"I still can't believe he didn't end up using his computer," said Maggie.

"I know," said Fenton. "I was pretty amazed, too. Although he did use it to do all his research. Which reminds me of another surprising thing Max said."

"What's that?" asked Maggie.

"That he wants to come back and visit Morgan again soon," said Fenton.

"Really?" said Willy. "I kind of got the feeling that Max didn't like it here so much."

"That's for sure," cracked Maggie. "If you ask me, Max belonged in Wyoming about as much as, as—"

"About as much as that dilophosaurus belonged in the Cretaceous," finished Fenton. "I know, I know. But I guess he must have realized that spending all his time in front of the computer made him kind of miss out on finding out what it was really like here."

"Yeah," said Willy. "Morgan's a really fun place."

"And thanks to Max, now it's more fun than ever," said Maggie. "After all, if it weren't for him, we wouldn't have this Ping-Pong table." She hammered the ball by Fenton. "That's twenty-one. I win again. Okay, Fen, your turn."

"Hey," said Fenton, taking the paddle from Willy, "how come you keep winning, Maggie?"

Jane put down her recorder. "I know why," she said.

"Why?" asked Willy, as Fenton served the ball.

"Because," said Jane proudly, "she's playing on *my* half of the Ping-Pong table."

They all laughed.

Fenton looked down at the ground again as he prepared to turn around and start his next row. As he did, he noticed that the rise where the trailer was perched was covered with rocks and gravel, and mixed in among it here and there were some interesting-looking, thin, hard, grayish chips.

Fenton bent down to look closer, wondering what the chips could be. They definitely didn't look like any pieces of bone he'd ever seen. Maybe they were fragments of some kind of rock. He reached down and picked one up.

The piece in his hand was about the size of a quarter. Its edges were jagged, and the surface was pebbly on one side, smooth on the other, and very slightly curved, almost like it had once been part of something round.

Then Fenton had a flash; if what he was thinking were true, this could be an amazing find!

He looked around wildly. As he did, he saw that, in fact, the rise that the trailer was on was actually a mound, an almost perfect circle, about ten feet across.

Suddenly, Fenton knew exactly what he was looking at.

"Dad! Charlie! Everyone! Come quick!" he yelled. "I think I just discovered a nest!"

Look for **DINOSAUR DETECTIVE #5** and the rest of the series in your local bookstore, or call the toll-free number 1-800-877-5351.

Join Fenton Rumplemayer in more of his awesome adventures
in the Dinosaur Detective series.

#1 On the Right Track

Fenton feels out of place when he first moves to Wyoming. But
when a mysterious set of dinosaur tracks turns up, he's right at
home. Hooked up by computer to his old pal Max in New York, and
ably assisted by a new friend, Fenton tackles a case that has the local
scientific team baffled.

#2 Fair Play

Fenton is the new kid in his class in Wyoming, and the bully has
chosen him to pick on. But Fenton and his new friend Maggie have a
great project for this year's Dinosaur Fair, and they're hot on the trail
of a fossil that's missing from his father's dinosaur dig. Can Fenton
and his friends find the missing piece, foil the bully, and still have
their project ready in time for the fair?

#3 Bite Makes Right

Can a dinosaur be part bird-hipped and part lizard-hipped?
That's sure what Professor Rumplemayer's new fossil find looks like.
Fenton is stumped. And on top of that he's been adopted by a stray
mutt that's making trouble for all of his friends. Can Fenton find a
good home for the dog and solve the mystery?

#4 Out of Place

Max, Fenton's computer-whiz pal, comes from New York for
Halloween. But the visit isn't as much fun as the boys expected. Max
doesn't get along with Fenton's new friends, and he thinks the story
of the town's founding is a big joke. He doesn't even like working at
the dig site, where the paleontologists have found a dinosaur that
seems misplaced in time.

Try some other dinosaur books from *Scientific American Books for Young Readers*—

Jack Horner: Living With Dinosaurs
by Don Lessem, from the new Science Superstars series.

Jack Horner found his first fossil when he was eight years old. From that day on, he knew exactly what he wanted to do when he grew up—study dinosaurs. But his dream looked like it was over after he flunked out of college—seven times!

Author Don Lessem, founder of the Dinosaur Society and a friend of Jack Horner's, tells the stranger-than-fiction story of a man who followed his own path to become one of the world's leading dinosaur experts, the real-life hero behind the scientist in the book and movie *Jurassic Park.*

Colossal Fossil
The Dinosaur Riddle Book by the Riddle King himself, Mike Thaler

- What dinosaur was a great boxer?

- What dinosaur played video games?

- What do you call a prehistoric Girl Scout?

Find the answers to these riddles and many more inside this wacky book about the most fascinating creatures to walk (shake?) the Earth.

#5 The Case of the Mystery Weekend

George and Pat are going to play "Sherlock Condo" and "Dr. Whatzit" at a Mystery Weekend Party. But one wrong turn leads them to Wit's End, a sinister mansion presided over by the butler, Peeved. Strange things begin to happen as the guests disappear one by one. Who extracted Kitty Feline, world-renowned dentist? Who snipped short the song of jazzman Miles Reed? And how did soap star Sally Storm slip away? Can George and Pat out-math the mastermind behind it all? DUM DEE DUM DUM.

#6 The Case of the Smart Dummy

It's a case of mistaken cases! Ventriloquist Edgar Bergman is dumbfounded when he loses his luggage with Lolly, his dummy, inside. Instead, he's left holding the bag, and it's full of stolen money. The only one who's talking is Edgar's other dummy, Charlie McShtick, and he says Edgar is innocent. Is Edgar in the act or can Pat and George find out who's pulling the strings? DUM DEE DUM DUM.